Anonymous

A black Prince

And other Stories

Anonymous

A black Prince
And other Stories

ISBN/EAN: 9783337172640

Printed in Europe, USA, Canada, Australia, Japan

Cover: Foto ©Andreas Hilbeck / pixelio.de

More available books at **www.hansebooks.com**

A BLACK PRINCE

And Other Stories

BY THE AUTHOR OF "TOLD IN THE VERANDAH."

SECOND EDITION.

LONDON
LAWRENCE & BULLEN
16 HENRIETTA STREET, COVENT GARDEN, W.C.
1893

NOTE.

Some of the stories in the present Volume have appeared in the *Madras Mail*. For permission to republish them I am indebted to the courtesy of the Editor. "A Black Prince," "How we Jubilated," and other papers are published for the first time.

CONTENTS.

MISS B——

ON a March evening, not many years ago, two young men were dining together at the South-Western Railway Hotel, Southampton. They were subalterns in a light cavalry regiment, and on the following morning were to embark for India to join.

Charlie Fancourt and Vyvian Dale were two of the best-looking youngsters in the service. Fate had been kind to them in various ways, but in the Victorian, as in the Augustan, age, black Care frequently sits on a cavalry crupper, and these young officers were not leaving their native land in that cheerful frame of mind which the call of duty should inspire.

"Hullo! you sportsmen! What have you done with Jack?"

The speaker had just entered the room, and, recognizing the young men, made his way to their table. He was an elderly man, short and thick-set, with a

B

bronzed face, lighted up by shrewd grey eyes, and as he had more than once been heard to declare, no safer man for a touch-and-go operation held a surgeon's commission in the mounted branch of the service than Hector Macnab.

"What's become of Jack?" he again inquired, after mutual greetings had been exchanged.

"Can't say; may have missed the train. Perhaps he has been nabbed by the Jews," was the careless reply.

"What, lucky Jack a bondsman to the Israelite! Fortunatus in fetters! No, I don't think *that's* likely," said the Doctor, laughing.

Macnab was right, it was not likely. Jack Smith was not without reason known throughout his brigade as "Lucky Jack." His good fortune was phenomenal. His star shone with a perennial lustre that reduced the luminaries of other men to the condition of ephemeral sparks. Out big-game shooting, his performances went nigh to rival the feats peculiar to the hero of a young lady's novel. If he essayed his chances at a lottery, men grew mournfully profane, for they held the result to be a foregone conclusion. He got his troop quicker than had been the case with any other lieutenant since the regiment was embodied, and he gained his V. C. by cantering out of action with the body of the man to whose vacancy he was afterwards promoted. But to recount every instance of the lucky Lancer's good fortune would lead my readers to believe me to be straying into the regions of romance.

"And what's the row with *you ?* " continued the Doctor : " down on your luck at parting with Polly ? Poor fellows ! what are you drinking ? " and without waiting for a reply he poured out half a tumblerful of champagne, and, heartily invoking luck upon the party, tossed off the gooseberry with a recklessness that denoted an advanced stage of thirst.

"We have been cursing the chosen people, Doctor," remarked Dale after a pause.

" Oh, that's the way the cat jumps ! Are you badly hit too, Fanny ? "

Fancourt nodded and Dale whistled carelessly.

" Well," said the Doctor, turning to Dale, with mock severity, " if I were your respected sire, Master Vyvian, I would cut you off with a bob and my blessing, and less too, if ropes were cheaper."

" Just what the governor said this morning." said Dale, " and I told him that as life in the East was uncertain, and I might not live to come into my coin,

I would have the shilling down, but he might keep his blessing till he saw fit to let Cox honour my cheques."

" And what does *your* Relieving Officer say, Fancourt ? " asked the elder man, after laughing at Dale's irreverence.

" I am to live on two hundred a year, till I get my troop, or go to——"

" To old Hornie ? Right, perfectly right," said the Doctor approvingly.

"No, to Queensland: much the same sort of thing I fancy, place where fellows live on tea and kangaroo."

" Very wholesome diet," replied Macnab, " cheap, and no gout in it. I'll tell you what you fellows should do," he suddenly remarked. The young men eyed him with an air of gloomy inquiry. " You should both of you *marry coin.*"

" I consider a man who marries for money a very poor sort of a sportsman," observed Dale.

" Fancy, having to ask your wife for pocket-money," remarked Fancourt, with lofty scorn.

" And having to tell her how you spend it," added Dale, with a laugh.

The Doctor lifted up his hand deprecatingly. " My dear boys—listen to me—listen, Fancourt. Doesn't the Laureate say, ' Proputty, proputty, prop——' "

"No, Macnab," broke in Dale, "never mind the Laureate, we must pull through without putting ourselves into the slave-market."

The conversation was here interrupted by a waiter who approached with a letter. "Either o' you gentlemen Dr. Nab?"

"Mac, if you please," answered the Doctor, with an air of dignity. "Yes, it is for me," and taking the missive, he broke the seal.

"Why, here's the very thing for you," he exclaimed, with sudden animation; "at least for one of you," he added. "Listen to this now. My friend Deedes — Deedes & Willes, attorneys, Lincoln's Inn—writes on business and winds up: 'You will have as a fellow-passenger Miss Bull—Butt—' *Bullion* it looks like, 'a relative of the G. G., who is being shipped off to Calcutta to get her out of the way of a detrimental. She has £30,000 a year under her late father's will, and as much more to follow when her mother dies—but they try to keep it dark to save her from fortune-hunters.' There's your chance, my beamish boys," cried the Doctor, with enthusiasm. "I only wish I hadn't a wife and five young Macnabs. Now go in one of you and win."

"Sixty thou' a year," murmured Dale contemplatively.

"What did you say her name is?" inquired Fancourt, with an appearance of awakening interest.

"Can't read it," said Macnab. "Deedes doesn't write copper-plate. 'Bullion' it can't be, no such name—appropriate to the lady though. Here, waiter, bring a list of passengers going by the *Rissaldar*."

There were only two single ladies whose names began with B—these were Miss Buller and Miss Butler. "Well, it's one of them," said Macnab. "It's for you to find out which. Don't fight over her."

"Wonder if she's pretty," mused Fancourt.

"Bet you she's as ugly as old boots," muttered Dale.

"All very rich women *are*," sighed the other.

"Never mind her face, my lads, think of her figure," said the Doctor sententiously. "Now, I'm off to roost—we sail at eight, remember."

As the Doctor left the room, a young lady of ordinary appearance and of homely habiliments, who had been dining by herself at an adjacent table, shot a penetrating glance at the subalterns, and, rising slowly, went into the sitting-room.

The young men descended to the hall, and lighted their cigars. They had exchanged barely a syllable since Macnab left them, and both appeared to be absorbed in reverie. As they put on their cover-coats preparatory to a post-prandial stroll, they simultaneously exclaimed—

" Deuced fortunate Jack Smith's not here ! "

The voyage commenced auspiciously. The *Rissaldar* was an excellent vessel. The passengers were agreeable people, the weather was delightful, and Jack Smith did not turn up, but at the last moment telegraphed to say that the sudden illness of a wealthy and venerable relative, concerning whom it was known that he cherished the most encouraging expectations, would detain him in England until the departure of the following steamer.

Thus the young soldiers felt that they had before them a clear field for whatever ventures their sense of the expedient might impel them to engage in. But for the first time during a long and intimate acquaintance the two friends became sensible of a restraint in one another's society, and, as though by tacit agreement, it soon fell out that they seldom found themselves together. They sat apart at meals, and even the nightly pipe, that bond and sacrament of good fellowship, was smoked with some other companion.

On the second evening after leaving Southampton, as Dale was sauntering on deck with the officer of the watch, the latter chanced to inquire whether Dale knew a lady on board named Butler. This was the plainly-dressed young lady whom we observed dining at the hotel. "They say," continued the sailor, " that the girl is hard hit about some smart fellow in England, and that her people are shipping her off to Calcutta for change of scene. She told Mrs. Cackle the whole story."

This was important news for Dale. It harmonized with one of the particulars related in Mr. Deedes' letter. It was a gleam of light, and he treasured it as a turf tout hugs a straight tip on a real good thing. The chances of travel had made Dale Miss Butler's *vis-à-vis* at table, and the practised eye of the Lancer had already noted that the lady's glance fell not unfrequently in the direction of his own good-looking face.

The day after his conversation with the ship's officer, he picked up the young lady's thimble for her and made its presentation the vehicle of a self-accomplished introduction. They discoursed upon the delightful weather and the graceful flight of the sea-gulls, and both agreed that aquamarine was a colour of unrivalled beauty. The damsel, who was as plain in feature as she was in raiment, held but little intercourse with the other passengers, and occupied herself from morning till night with some abstruse description of needlework; occasionally, but that was in the absence of Dale, she amused herself with a novel. It is needless, therefore, to say that the sagacious soldier at once found himself in easy and unchallenged possession.

Miss Buller was a being of a very different order. She was a strikingly handsome girl, and everything about her, from her boots to her brilliants, betokened wealth as plainly as Miss Butler's surroundings indicated poverty.

She was vivacious and sociable, and talked fluently about the doings of the upper ten thousand. Her diamonds and emeralds were displayed perhaps a little more copiously than good taste might desire, but then she had small and well-shaped hands, and the rings suited them.

Fancourt regarded her at first critically, then approvingly, and at last admiringly. He was satisfied that the heiress was not Dale's friend, and that the prize could consequently be none other than Miss Buller. Yet at times he was sorely perplexed.

He was a past-master in all that relates to the ways of women, and his experience, deep and comprehensive though it was, afforded him no instance of a well-born girl of enormous wealth and no little beauty, who had been out in the world for some time—Miss Buller confessed to three seasons—and had yet been suffered to complete the term of her legal infancy without the tutelary interposition of a husband *in esse* or *in posse*. But after long and anxious deliberation he came to the conclusion that the young lady in question formed a brilliant and unique exception to the general rule. She was a Koh-i-noor among maidens, and Lieutenant Fancourt was her discoverer. But was he destined ever to wear this radiant gem ? Alas ! rumours were soon busy about the ship, rumours that occasioned him the utmost disquietude, for he was not the only captivator of dames on board, and attention to Miss Buller became exasperatingly general when it was whispered that she already counted her income by lacs, and in the not far distant future would reckon it by crores.

It is to be suspected that this report had its origin in certain unguarded confidences with which Surgeon-Major Macnab had favoured the ship's doctor over a

very late glass of whisky-toddy on the night following their departure from Southampton ; but to
whatever cause it may be attributed, the competition
for Miss Buller's good graces soon became strenuous
and unremitting.

A young Indian Civilian (first of his year), of
undeniable classical attainments, celebrated the
lady's charms in several beautiful choriambic pen-
tameters, which he handed to her one morning after
breakfast; and a stalwart gentleman from the
Antipodes fervently urged upon her acceptance a
well-matched team of chestnut thorough-breds, foaled
on his own run, and schooled with his own hands ;
but as the verses were in Latin, and the coursers were
in Queensland, these otherwise formidable overtures
proved in no degree prejudicial to the interests of the
young Lancer, who, notwithstanding all opposition,
and in spite of occasional moonlight strolls and quiet
chats in secluded corners, half-scornfully conceded to
deluded rivals, was soon installed as first favourite,
and permitted steadily to improve his advantage.

By the time the *Rissaldar* anchored at Valetta,
Fancourt and Dale were friends again. They never
alluded even remotely to the subject of heiresses, but
spoke to one another in a vague, dreamy sort of way

about the superiority of the settled life of a married
man, to the chequered and aimless existence of a
bachelor. Sometimes they would become slightly
metaphysical, and one would solemnly remark that
affinities were deuced uncommonly curious things,
and the other would nod gravely and moralize upon
the wonderful influence that Fate has over a fellow's
destiny. And so the happy days sped by, while the
big toiling ship was ever steadily ploughing her way
eastward to the now not distant goal.

It was a charming moonlight night; the sky
glittered like Streeter's shop-window on a bright June
morning; the sea was as smooth as the pavement of
Pall Mall, and the keel of the good ship was as steady
as the foundations of Westminster Abbey. It was
the last night of the voyage, and the passengers had
retired to bed early in order to prepare themselves for
the labours of the morrow.

The deck was deserted save by four people who
formed two couples, one of which lingered at the
stern, gazing down at the ship's coruscating track,
while the other loitered at the bulwarks, and directed
romantic glances towards the star-girt moon.

"Do you honestly despise wealth and position?"
asked a soft voice at the stern.

"And you really love me for myself alone?" rippled from a rosebud mouth at the bulwarks.

A malicious twinkle gleamed from out the stellar depths, and the infusoria broke into a thousand laughing sparkles in the vessel's wake. The answers, audible only to her to whom they were addressed, were accompanied by precisely the same action; an arm encircled the waist of the querist, and a long unresisted kiss terminated the dialogue. "*Safe!*" was the triumphant ejaculation uttered in the inmost recesses of at least three quickly beating hearts. The stars smiled with a chilly astral sneer; the giddy molecules rolled over and over in a delirium of spiteful glee; while a little cloud that had been hovering above the moon dropped across it for a moment like the lid of a winking eye.

Three days after the *Rissaldar* had glided to her moorings at Mazagon, two marriages were celebrated in that remarkable arrangement of masonry which the inhabitants of Bombay accept as a Cathedral, and the local journals in their next issue contained the following items of domestic intelligence:—

"On the 1st of April. at the Cathedral, Bombay, by the Rev. Joyne Handes: Vyvian Dale, Lieut., Royal Ruby Lancers, to Sarah Butler, eldest daughter of the late Patrick

Arminius Butler, Esq., of Dublin : and at the same time and place, Charles Medows Stanley Fancourt, Lieut., Royal Ruby Lancers, to Florence Imogen Clarissa, sole surviving daughter of Horace Fitzroy Buller, Esq., formerly of Belgrave Square, London, and of the Grange, East Bulsted, Kent."

On the following day they all started for Jehannum, where the " Rubies " were in garrison.

" Now which of you two fellows has got the plum ?" asked the Doctor, in a stage whisper, as the three men were taking their tickets at the Boree Bunder Railway Station.

" Don't know, and don't care," was the ready response.

" Love in a cottage for *one* of you," said Macnab, pursing his mouth.

" You're always so beastly mercenary, Macnab."

But as they spoke the young men in their hearts respected the worldly wisdom of their senior, and each felt a vague sort of pity for the other.

The Lancers had a capital Mess. Their Bungalow was by far the coolest building in Jehannum, which, as every well-informed person knows, is a proverbially hot station ; and the pleasantly-shaded ante-room, with its large punkahs and well-watered window-mats, was a favourite afternoon lounge on the days when the English mail came in.

On the first pay-day after their arrival at their new station the young Benedicts went with a light heart into a committee of ways and means with their respective wives. It was the first time that reference had been made in either establishment to the not unimportant subject of supply.

* * * *

An hour or two later Fancourt strolled into the ante-room of the Lancers' Mess with a gloomy, not to say despairing, expression on his usually serene features : his hands were thrust deep into his trousers pockets, and his white teeth were set with vicious energy on the stump of an extinct cheroot. As he entered the room he met Dale, who looked as though he had just received sentence of death.

" Wish you joy, Dale,"

" Congratulate you, Fancourt."

There was a painful want of cordiality in their greetings, and for a moment they glared at one another fiercely.

" What the devil do you mean ? " was the reciprocal and discourteous rejoinder.

Dale was the first to speak. " I have just discovered that my wife has not got a penny, so yours possesses £30,000 a year, which," he added icily, " I suppose is a subject for congratulation."

" Mrs. Dale without a penny !—Is *she* not the heiress ? " asked Fancourt slowly.

" The *heiress*, my dear fellow !—you know perfectly well she's not ! " was the angry reply.

Fancourt appeared to be utterly bewildered, but after a short pause resumed : " *My* wife told me this afternoon that her father had just gone through the Court, and that she was being sent out to live with an uncle in a Sepoy regiment."

" And Mrs. Dale," said the other, with a bitter laugh, " was coming out in connection with a Zenana mission."

" Mail's in ! " cried Macnab, bustling into the room followed by the Mess-Sergeant carrying a bundle of newspapers. "Hullo!" exclaimed the Doctor, glancing down the columns of the *Home News*. " Did you *ever* hear of such luck ? Just like him ! Listen :— ' Miss Bulteel, the great Warwickshire heiress, who was about to proceed to India on a visit to her relative the Governor-General, is engaged to be married to Captain John Smith, V.C., Royal Ruby Lancers. The circumstances attending the engagement are of a highly romantic character. Miss Bulteel and Captain

Smith, who, we understand, were then perfect
strangers, had taken their passage to Bombay
by the SS. *Rissaldar*, but being prevented by
unforeseen circumstances from sailing in that
vessel, both of them made arrangements to
proceed to India in the following steamer. Miss
Bulteel proposed to join the ship in the Solent,
embarking from her uncle Lord Spynnacre's yacht,
but the day being stormy, it was with the utmost
difficulty that the yacht's boat could be brought
alongside the steamer. In ascending the ladder
the young lady slipped and fell into the sea,
while at the same moment a large wave capsized the
boat, rendering all aid from that quarter impossible.
Miss Bulteel would, in all human probability, have
perished, had not the gallant Smith, who was viewing
the scene from the steamer's deck, immediately leaped
into the water and supported the half-drowned lady,
until a boat was lowered. Gratitude to her brave
preserver soon ripened into a warmer feeling, and
before they arrived at Gibraltar they had become
engaged. They returned to England by the next
homeward-bound mail-boat, and preparations are
already in progress for the celebration of the wedding
early in the autumn. It is reported in military

C

circles that Captain Smith sends in his papers and
retires from the service.'"

"*Whew!*" whistled the worthy Doctor, looking
compassionately at the two blank faces before him;
"well, at any rate, you both get a step; and, after all,
the young woman would have been thrown away
upon either of *you*, as it is not your form to *marry
money*, don't ye see?"

There was an interval of silence. Neither of the
younger men had any remark to offer; one sat with
his gaze fixed upon the ceiling, the other with his
eyes riveted upon the floor—their legs were stretched
out to the farthest length, and their hands were
buried in their pockets. The Doctor continued
imperturbably: "You see, you fellows married for
love"—the miserable subalterns winced—"and quite
right too—that is to say, regarding life from *your*
point of view; but," he added, with a wicked twinkle
of the eye, and a sly shake of the head, "I think,
taking all that you have told me into consideration,
that if I had been in *your* place, my dear boys, I
should have been mean enough to go in for coin.
Mess-boy, bring me a peg."

BURNT FINGERS.

A BEAUTIFUL young woman stood gazing at the sun as it sank in a confused glory of orange and purple behind the mountain barrier that shields the little hill-station of Baowao from the fury of the summer monsoon. Lounging carelessly by her side was a middle-aged man of small stature and homely features. He carried a stout umbrella, and was arrayed in garments of the subdued tint affected by the Indian cleric out for a holiday.

During some moments neither of them spoke. The silence was at length broken by an exclamation from the lady.

"Oh, *John !* how foolish of me ! I have dropped my sunshade."

They were leaning over the parapet of a lichen-covered stone bridge which spanned a narrow but deep gully, along which a shallow stream babbled among tangled undergrowth and boulders. Halfway down the bank grew a small guava-tree, from a straggling branch of which the sunshade was now helplessly suspended.

" Allow me to get it for you."

The tones were deep and musical. Now, John's articulation was void of melody, and the voice clearly was not his. The lady turned her head and saw a stranger in the act of lightly vaulting over the parapet. He returned in a moment, and as he gave her the sunshade he bowed with the easy grace of a finished squire of dames. He was a tall, good-looking fellow of the rakish heavy dragoon order, which, according to a certain eminent lady-novelist, typifies all that is excellent in man.

" Lovely evening," he remarked. " Have you just come up ? "

" We arrived this morning," replied John.

" Staying at the hotel ? "

" No; we have taken a little house called ' Eglantine,' near the church."

" Ah, yes, I know the place, little house with a gable. I shall, with your permission, do myself the honour of calling upon you. Good evening," and with an admiring glance at John's companion, the interesting stranger gracefully lifted his sombrero and strolled away.

The next day being Sunday, the new arrivals attended church, and the entire station spent the remainder of the afternoon in discussing them.

It was discovered at the Post-Office that their name was Birt, and it was stated, with some show of authority, that the gentleman was a Nonconformist minister; this statement was at once accepted, all conflicting theories being excluded by the stranger's appearance and demeanour. Opinion, however, was not so united regarding the personal attributes of the lady. The men with one voice declared her to be the handsomest woman it had been the good fortune of Baowao to behold for years; but the ladies found a something in her eyes, or her mouth, or her nose, or her expression that was hopelessly inconsistent with any well-founded claim to real beauty. But it was ever the same —from the day when Lilith criticized the newly-arrived Eve, and the world first heard the accents of detraction.

On the following morning, as Mrs. Birt was sitting in her little verandah attempting to sketch the peak of Mount Marguerite, which formed the most promi

nent object in the landscape before her, a card was
brought in :—

CAPTAIN LORRAINE,
40th Hussars.

She handed it to her husband, remarking that it
probably appertained to the obliging gentleman that
had rescued her sunshade at the bridge.

She was right.   Captain Lorraine had promised to
call, and he was a man who scrupulously fulfilled all
engagements of that nature when made with a pretty
woman.

The visit was not of long duration, and the talk
was of the commonplace order peculiar to first calls;
but the gallant soldier went home strangely discom-
posed, and with a confused vision of two small black
brodequins and a pair of large blue eyes, which
rendered him unusually contemplative during the
remainder of the day.

Some portion of the result of the Captain's reflections may be gathered from the subjoined letter which
arrived at ' Eglantine ' a day or two after this interview :—

"THE NEST, *Wednesday.*

" DEAR MR. BIRT—Will you and Mrs. Birt give me the
pleasure of your company at a little picnic which I am getting
up for to-morrow.   We are going to the large Cascade, and

ride by the Upper Road. I will send ponies for you both, and will, if you allow me, act as your pioneer.

"Yours very truly,

"VICTOR LORRAINE."

The picnic was a delightful outing. Mr. Birt happened to have brought his own pony, but the Captain's offer of a mount was thankfully accepted on behalf of the lady.

Lorraine was assiduous in his solicitude for their comfort throughout the day; and seeing that Mr. Birt was deeply engaged with a cheroot and a brandy-and-soda, the Captain, with his usual thoughtfulness, offered to show Mrs. Birt the famous view of the Cascade, which is seen to such advantage from the opposite side of the torrent ; but, after crossing by the stepping-stones to the other bank, he was doubtless much gratified to find that Mr. Birt had silently joined them, and that the " Padre " therefore would not be deprived of the pleasure which that charming prospect never fails to afford a stranger.

After this Mr. Birt attended his wife so closely throughout the day that the obliging Captain found it impossible to show her even a tree-fern or a wild bee's nest without the escort of the faithful John.

The picnic was much enjoyed by all, except perhaps by the host, who appeared to be suffering from some concealed vexation; and when a comparison of watches placed it beyond doubt that the time had arrived to set out for home, the regrets were eloquent and universal.

Captain Lorraine, owing to the exigencies presented by a narrow bridle-path, found himself on the return journey riding in the rear of the column with an elderly lady, of high local rank, who detained him as her escort until he was called away by a sudden confusion at the head of the line.

Mr. Birt's pony was obstinately refusing to pass a fallen tree that lay across the road, leaving but a narrow passage between its farthermost branches and a precipice. The animal had passed it in the morning without trouble, but not liking the aspect from this side, reared, snorted, and showed unmistakable signs of vicious and determined refusal.

In vain his rider plied both heels and umbrella, the steed had hardened its heart, and Mr. Birt was compelled to draw up on one side and let his more comfortably mounted companions proceed. When all had gone by, Captain Lorraine, who had promptly taken the vacant place by the side of Mrs. Birt—she looked more lovely than ever in her anxiety for John's safety—cheerfully called out to the "Padre" that they were only three miles from home, and that as soon as they got back, he would send a quiet pony for the derelict, and a syce to bring home the refractory animal by the lower road.

Mr. Birt, however, not relishing the prospect of an hour's delay upon the *ghât*, slowly trotted his pony back for some fifty yards, and, suddenly turning its stubborn little head, came down towards the gap at a smart canter. On approaching the opening the pony, either swerving or yielding to an impulse communicated by its rider, went straight as an arrow at the prostrate trunk and cleared the timber like a deer.

"Well done!" shouted Lorraine, with a touch of disappointment in his tone, "you must run that pony of yours for the Baowao Cup, Mr. Birt."

"All right," was the reply, "you can enter him for me if you like."

"Owners up, you know," said Lorraine, with a quizzical smile.

"I'm agreeable," said Mr. Birt resignedly, "so long as it's not owners down."

They all laughed at the little joke, and that

evening Lorraine entered the pony for the steeple-
chase.

The Captain shared his Bungalow with a young
gentleman of his own regiment, who was known
among his familiars as " the Boy." To this appella-
tion the Baowao ladies had seen fit to add a qualifica-
tion, and called him "the Pretty Boy," but his name
stood recorded in the Army List as Thomas Latchford.

Observing that, since the picnic, his chum had
been gradually lapsing into despondency, and readily
divining the cause, the sagacious subaltern proposed
to his senior that they should give a tennis-party
followed by a small and early dance.

The suggestion was adopted with alacrity, and the
Captain, restored and comforted, again betook himself to pen and ink. On this occasion, however, he
confined himself to the inscription of a few words
upon a card :—

" Captain Lorraine and Mr. Latchford at home.

" Monday, 15th May.

" Lawn-Tennis, Dancing.

"The Nest."   "R.S.V.P."

The above, after several transcripts of it had been
made by Latchford, was placed in one of the Captain's

best envelopes and carefully directed in that officer's own hand to Mrs. Birt, who on behalf of herself and the faithful John graciously accepted the invitation.

The party was attended by all the station, for the occupants of "The Nest" were as popular as they were hospitable, and the gaieties of Baowao were not so numerous as to clash one with another.

Considerable diversion was occasioned by the awkwardness displayed in the tennis-court by Mr. Birt, who was not a proficient in the popular game, but all allowed that the light and graceful waltzing of his wife in the dance that followed left nothing to be desired even by the most fastidious.

"The Boy," who was no mean performer in his pumps, was Mrs. Birt's most favoured partner; while the elder warrior, now more dejected than ever, was obliged to content himself with the well-meaning but ponderous pirouetting of a local belle, who more than once took occasion to remark to her mournful cavalier that she could not understand what the men saw to rave about in that milk-and-water child, Mrs. Birt.

When the two Hussars met the next day at a very late breakfast, Captain Lorraine gloomily congratulated his junior on the good luck that had befallen him on the previous evening. " You made great running with Mrs. B., Tom," he observed, as he wearily cracked an egg.

" I did *so*, old fellow," replied the ingenuous Boy; " I had five dances with her off the reel, and what's more, she's asked me to dine with them to-morrow."

The Captain dropped his egg-spoon and stared long and sternly at the favoured subaltern: his feelings then found vent in a subdued whistle.

After the night of the dance Latchford dined frequently at " Eglantine," and something in the nature of a coldness gradually arose between the two comrades in arms. Luckily, however, for their mutual friend-ship, Lorraine, who was the Honorary Secretary to the Gymkhana, was during the next few days too busily employed in making arrangements for the coming race-meeting to brood over the caprices of fortune and the vanity of human wishes.

It was remarked by those who paid attention to such matters that the jumps on this occasion were much stiffer than usual; and, moreover, that for the first time in the history of the meeting a repulsive-looking double formed one of the obstacles.

On the morning of the race all the station met at the little library to make up their books and discuss the coming events.

Captain Lorraine, a betting-book in his hand and a pencil between his teeth, was absorbed in abstruse calculations. " Will you back your mount, Mr. Birt ? " he asked, as that gentleman entered the room ; " I'll give you ten to one."

" Ten to one, eh ?—ten to one. What in ? "

" Mohurs or rupees, just as you like," replied the Captain carelessly.

" Oh, do bet gold-mohurs, John," cried Mrs. Birt ; " you know how I want a coin necklace."

" Mohurs, then," said John.

" Tens or hundreds ? " asked Lorraine. He was getting angry, and felt inclined to plunge.

" Hundreds," answered John, with sturdy resolution, as he proceeded to book the bet in a dropsical old pocket-book.

There was a large gathering to witness the races. Planters rode in from all quarters, and many people came up from the plains, for the Baowao pony-meeting afforded a very pleasant holiday.

Before the great event of the day came off, several flat races and a match were run, and while these minor matters were in progress, Mr. Birt, umbrella in hand and cheroot in mouth, sauntered quietly round the steeple-chase course.

He lingered a little at the double, and the faintest trace of a smile played over his solemn features as his eye fell upon the stalwart form of the Honorary Secretary towering among a distant group of ladies.

There were five entries for the steeplechase, and each animal was ridden by its owner. The following was the list :—

Captain Lorraine's	b. a. p. 11st. 12 lbs.	..The Pet.
Mr. Latchford's	ch. a. p. 9st. 7 lbs.	...Monkey.
„ Noakes'	g. ch. p. 10st.	...Indigo.
„ Stokes'	bl. ch. p. 10st. 3lbs.	...Lightning.
„ Birt's	ch. aus. p. 9st.	...Kangaroo.

When the ponies assembled at the starting-post, Captain Lorraine looked with profound surprise, not unmingled with dismay, at Mr. Birt, who, in his racing dress, wore a very different appearance from the semi-clerical John of private life.

That gentleman now wore colours that once were dark blue, but by much hard work had been worn to a serviceable brown; his tops and breeches were unexceptionable, but his jockey cap still carried an old stain which spoke of too close a contact with mother earth. His keen grey eyes flashed with demure roguery, and his saturnine face beamed as though with the light of coming pleasure.

Kangaroo was a picture of racing form; and his rider, as he brought him into line, looked from cap to spur a horseman.

Mr. Birt nodded good-humouredly to " the Boy," and told him to sit fast at the double.

" Rein back there ! Steady a bit on the left— go ! ! ! "

At the first fence there was a sudden fall in *Indigo ;* at the water Mr. Stokes performed a remarkable feat of acrobatic horsemanship, clearing the brook all by himself; but as probably he was a bad conductor, *Lightning* remained on the other side. Birt then found himself alone with the two Hussars. Both his opponents rode well, and their ponies, which were above the average, had been carefully schooled. Lorraine lay a little behind, but " the Boy " kept *Monkey* well abreast of *Kangaroo.* Mr. Birt now slightly forced the pace, and brought Latchford up to a stone wall a trifle quicker than that astute young gentleman would have travelled had he not been afraid of losing touch of *Kangaroo,* whose rider took a pull just in time to steady him for the jump. The result was as Birt had intended : *Monkey* shot a-head and fell, and although " the Boy " was soon in the saddle again, the course was so short that he was practically out of the race. Lorraine now came up and raced Birt neck and neck to the double, both entered it together, but Birt left it by himself. It was too stiff for the *Pet*, good beast though he was, to get out of with such a welter weight as Lorraine. *Kangaroo* having thus squandered the field, romped home an easy winner by several lengths, the panting and perspiring *Monkey* struggling in gamely, a very indifferent second. . . . .

Mr. Birt left Baowao after an exceedingly profitable settling-day; for, in addition to his heavy bet with Lorraine, he had, before dressing for the race, backed *Kangaroo* extensively: the "Padre's" general appearance, and especially his umbrella, inducing the confiding highlanders to give him more satisfactory odds than would have been obtainable had the dark sportsman been seen in his racing colours.

As he walked, gingham in hand, down the *ghât*, followed by Mrs. Birt on *Kangaroo*, and a train of coolies carrying their baggage, he ever and anon hummed softly to himself a few lines of a good old English song which has for its simple refrain the words: "I'm a young man from the country, but you don't get over *me*."

*   *   *   *

A few days after Mr. Birt's departure, a Major Hamilton of the 40th arrived at Baowao and put up with his brother-officers at " The Nest." As the three sat smoking and talking about the race-meeting the Major remarked : " So you have had Jack Birt and his pony up here ; of course, you had no chance for the Cup."

" And who the mischief *is* Jack Birt ? " asked Lorraine, with much interest.

" Birt," replied Hamilton, " is the new Waler jock. Haven't you heard about him ? He has come over to ride for the Rajah of Skurri. The pony was well known in Melbourne. They called it over there the Curate's Cob. Birt, you may have noticed, looks more like a parson than a jockey."

The Captain changed the conversation.

* * * *

" Vic, old boy, will you lend me a thou' ? " asked Latchford, as he and Lorraine were winding up their affairs at the close of their leave.

" I'm pretty well cleared out by Mr. Birt," said Lorraine, " but I think I can manage it. Can't you write a cheque, though ? You are well enough known up here."

"No use," said "the Boy" ruefully. "Birt had a cheque for all my balance at Tinny's."

"Bets?" laconically inquired Lorraine.

"No—*écarté*," murmured Latchford, almost blushing. "You see, whenever I dined up there I played *écarté* after dinner with Mrs. B., while Birt looked on; he said he never touched cards, it was against his principles. Madame, though, was a nailer at it, and she had the luck of the very d——l in holding the king."

SERGEANT SPELTER.

" DESERTERS are easy enough, they mostly all get into civilians' dress, and then they're nabbed." The speaker was Mr. Robert Runnymead, formerly an Inspector of the Madras City Police. He spoke with an air of authority, and I felt that I was conversing with an expert.

" You mean," said I, " that their military bearing betrays them."

" Exactly so. I once caught two of them by going into a railway-station waiting-room, on suspicion like, and suddenly shouting 'attention,' when up jumps a couple of gunners that had made a run of it from Mhow. They pretended they'd got up just to look at the clock.

" I suppose there is not much difficulty when they wear uniform ? " I remarked.

" Well, there ought not to be; but I've had my

disappointments in deserters as in most other things. I recollect once being nicely sold by a deserter.

"Ten or fifteen years ago a good many of them used to make their way down to the seaport towns, and if they could once manage to get on board ship they were pretty safe; for we couldn't wire after them as they do now, there being no submarine cable in those days.

"I was in charge of the B division at the time, and as I had the roadstead under me, I caught a tidy few of them as they tried to slip through. In fact, my name stood rather high in the force in the matter of deserters. I used to be called in the Department, Inspector Run-'em-in—ha! ha! Run-'em-in was what they used to call me. So when I read one morning that Richard Spayne, Quarter-Master Sergeant of the Hallamshire Buffs, had bolted with a large sum of money, and that five hundred rupees had been offered by the civil authorities for his capture—for it seems that he had committed some offence under the Penal Code as well—I said to myself, 'Well, Sergeant Spayne, if you find your way to Madras you're booked to me.'

"That afternoon, as I was writing up my diary, a bit of paper was brought to me with the words

'Sergeant Spelter, H.M.'s Hallamshire Light Infantry' written on it. So I put my work aside and told the boy to show the Sergeant in.

"My visitor was a very intelligent-looking man, and, in point of fact, was about as knowing as they're made. He handed me a chit from the Commissioner stating that the bearer was Sergeant Spelter, of the Hallamshires, who had come down in search of deserter Spayne, and I was to help him, and let him have a police-boat and so forth. I didn't like this; I felt that it was interfering with my natural work; besides, you see, there was five hundred rupees on it; the rupee was then at par, and fifty pounds was a consideration with me in those days—in fact, I don't know the time when it has not been a consideration. However, I had to be civil to the fellow, so I told him to sit down, and I gave him a cheroot and a drink, and tried to get something out of him, but he was close, close as wax. He evidently wanted that five hundred rupees as much as I did, and I could hardly get so much as a description of Spayne out of him. The roll sent from the Orderly Room was very incomplete, and would have applied to a hundred men in any regiment you like to name. In point of fact, Spelter himself was not unlike

Spayne, only Spelter's hair was black, and Spayne's was red, and Spelter's manner was soft and silky, and Spayne's was said to be rough and rude.

"I tell you I began to get a bit shirty with him at last, and it struck me that it wouldn't be a bad move to run *him* in—on suspicion you know, only on suspicion—and keep him till I had nabbed Spayne, when I could say, 'So sorry — over-zeal—stupid mistake,' and all that. I wish now I had done it, for Spelter was one too many for me in the end.

"'Well, Sergeant,' I said at last, 'I will give you all the help I can; you can have a boat whenever you want it. Do you require local information of any kind to start with?'

"'What steamers are in the roads?' he asked, careless like.

"'None. The *Khatmandoo* sailed this morning. We sha'n't have another in for a week.'

"'I know about the *Khatmandoo*,' he replied; 'she went an hour before I arrived, or I would have gone aboard,' and he seemed a bit put out to have missed her.

"'Well, Sergeant,' I said, 'you come and see me to-morrow and I'll tell you all I can gather;' but I meant to tell him just as much as I chose and no more.

" He then asked me to recommend him a quiet hotel, so I took him round to the Strasburg; and as he was a stranger in Madras, and had little or nothing in the way of luggage with him, the landlord wanted a guarantee, so I stood security for his expenses. This was going a little beyond what the Commissioner had ordered, but I knew that we could arrange matters afterwards with the regimental Adjutant.

" A week passed, and the Sergeant and I met every day. Each time that he called upon me he wanted a drink and a smoke, and then he had a way of always getting me to lend him something or other: one morning he borrowed five rupees; another day he asked for the loan of an umbrella; the next time he came he marched away with a box of my best cheroots; but he never had any news to give, and I began to think that Spayne must have slipped off in the *Khatmandoo*, or, maybe, had made for some other port.

" At last two steamers came into the roads: the *Emu*, for Ceylon and Australia, and the *Lady Nisbett*, for Calcutta.

" I knew that if Spayne was hiding anywhere in Madras this would bring him out, so I had all my men on the alert. I posted a Sergeant and three men

on the pier, and another with a party on the fore-
shore; a third I sent to the *Lady Nisbett*, while I
myself went on board the *Emu*, where I remained
for four-and-twenty mortal hours, and left only when
the mails came on board.

"Not a single one among the passengers or the
ship's company had escaped my eye, and I was satisfied that the *Emu* didn't hold the man.

"As I went down the side, up dashed a police-
boat with Sergeant Spelter in it. He was smoking
one of my cheroots and sitting under my umbrella.   I
shook my head and shouted, 'No go; he's not on
board, and they're just off.'   In fact, the lascars were
standing by, ready to haul up the ladder.

"'I've certain information that he has left the
shore,' said Spelter, as he ran up the side.

"If so, he's on board the *Lady Nisbett*, I thought,
but I only said, 'They'll take you to Ceylon, Spelter.'

"'Don't care if they do, so long as they take
Spayne too,' he cried.

"As soon as he got on deck the ladder was pulled
up, the screw began to move, and the ship steamed
out to sea.

"Thank the Lord! I thought; at any rate he's out

of the way, and now I have a free hand. The *Lady Nisbett* had her blue Peter flying, so I boarded her at once and had a good look round; but no one answering in the smallest particular to Spayne was among either passengers or crew.

"I remained in the vessel till she sailed, and as I and my Sergeant went on shore we had a real hearty laugh, I can tell you, over the trap Spelter had run his clever head into.

"That evening I got a note from the landlord of the Strasburg to say that Sergeant Spelter had forgotten to pay his bill; the account was enclosed, and, believe me, it was a startler. The man drank champagne-cup for early tea, and as for whisky, he must have bathed in it. There was a tidy sum, too, to pay for carriage-hire, and he had borrowed the landlord's watch and chain. A queer sort of a Sergeant, I thought, to send after a deserter; but I supposed the regimental authorities knew what they were about.

"The next day I got an order to attend at the Commissioner's office. When I entered the Colonel's private room with the hotel-bill in the heel of my fist, I saw a non-commissioned officer in the Hallamshire uniform standing at attention in front of the table ; he was in the middle of a statement, and I halted in the doorway so as not to interrupt him.

" ' He dyed his hair and whiskers black, your honour,' he was saying, ' and he deserted with his full Sergeant's uniform, and wherever he went he gave out that he was on the track of deserter Spayne. He gave a new name at every place he went to : I believe in Madras he called himself Spelter.'

" The Colonel looked at me, and I looked at the Colonel."

" What did the Colonel say ? " I asked.

The old Inspector's eye twinkled.

" Never mind, sir, what the Colonel *said;* he paid the bill."

"WHO WAS MRS. DUBERSOME?"

EVERYBODY knew who *Mr.* Dubersome was. The last-joined Civilian could have told you that he was first in Council at Fort St. George or, in the quaint phraseology of our native fellow-subjects, "the Second Governor;" and the better informed could have added that he was a son of Jack Dubersome, late Judge of the twenty-four Pergunnahs, whom his contemporaries, in a spirit of delicate irony, dubbed "Truthful John."

Although Mr. Dubersome was far too astute a man to earn for himself any such equivocal sobriquet as that borne by his father, it must be admitted that he was in no degree remarkable for his candour, and that he had a way of so managing his speech as to carry his frugality of the truth to the confines of avarice.

It need not be said that from such a man it was difficult to gather more of a subject than he thought fit to impart to you. So when after an unbroken sojourn of more than thirty years in the Carnatic he suddenly departed westward on three months' privilege leave, and returned at the expiration of that period with a wife, people waited in painful anxiety for some indication from him to satisfy their curiosity as to the lady's connections, fortune, and position, and the circumstances in which he had become acquainted with her.

But John Dubersome made no sign, and as the lady herself was equally uncommunicative, society resorted to conjecture; the logical basing their theories upon inference, while the merely imaginative raised airy structures upon romance.

Some of the ladies expressed their absolute conviction that they had seen the new *burra Mem Sahib* before—but where?—ah! where?

The men shook their heads sapiently, and wondered where old Dubersome could have picked her up.

Doctor Cockle did not scruple to aver that she must have been a hospital nurse; while clever Captain Macready, of dramatic fame, held it to be self-evident that she had been upon the stage: "In the provinces, don't you know."

Mrs. Argus concurred in the latter opinion;

perhaps she was influenced therein by the belief that such an extraction would not only impeach the new-comer's social position, but might at the same time reflect vaguely on her moral character. She there-fore arranged a little plan with the adroit Captain by means of which their pleasant hypothesis might be brought to the proof.

But *where* had Mr. Dubersome met the woman? It was established to the satisfaction of all that he had not made her acquaintance in England; for it was no secret that his wanderings had not extended beyond the little town of Sion in Switzerland, where he was laid up with a sharp attack of bronchitis; and what would a hospital nurse, or an actress during the height of the London season, be doing in an obscure village in the Canton of Valais?

The scheme concocted by Mrs. Argus and the histrionic Captain was to persuade Mrs. Dubersome to assist at some amateur theatricals got up for the occasion, in which a leading part was to be assigned to the stranger, when it would be evident from the manifest superiority of her acting that she was a genuine daughter of Thespis.

" You will detect it in a moment," declared the Captain, "by her manner of pronouncing *e a r*—

all her tears will be 'teeers,' and all her dears,
'deeers.' "

Mrs. Dubersome good-naturedly accepted the Captain's invitation, but warned him, with a smile on her
comely face, that she could not assure him that she
would not be overcome by stage-fright, for she had
never acted in her life.

The politic emissary of Mrs. Argus smirked
benignly, and said that he had not the slightest mis-
giving as to her success.

The play selected was the " Lady of Lyons," and
Mrs. Dubersome was cast for the heroine.

Expectation was at its height; the place that did
duty for a theatre was crowded; Captain Macready
excelled himself in his efforts to play up to Mrs.
Dubersome, and was well supported by the rest of the
company. In the centre seat of the second row sat
Mrs. Argus, her keen eyes assisted by a pair of
powerful opera-glasses, intently fixed upon the
débutante : but when the curtain fell, the general
verdict was that a more wooden and uninteresting
Pauline could not have been found within the confines
of broad Asia. Nevertheless Mrs. Argus was more
than ever convinced that Captain Macready was right :
" The woman is a born actress," she exclaimed, as

she swept from the hall, "only instead of giving us *Pauline* she was playing the part of *Agnes*."

Popular belief, however, now inclined to the view propounded by Dr. Cockle, upon whom all eyes were turned for a solution of the distressing problem, for society was beginning plaintively to tell itself that Mr. Dubersome had taken a cruelly unfair advantage of it, and had introduced something contraband into its sacred circle.

The Doctor was a man of infinite resource, and before long he informed Mr. Dubersome that the medical authorities were getting up an ambulance class, and that if Mrs. Dubersome would kindly consent to join it, her example he felt sure would be followed by others, and the movement would be safely inaugurated.

Mrs. Dubersome was delighted to have an opportunity of acquiring a knowledge of nursing. It was so useful; she would certainly join the class, only she hoped the Doctor would not expect her to cut up dead people : this she really could not undertake to perform, even as an amateur.

The Doctor amply reassured her upon this point, and in the course of a few days he had organized a large class of ladies, not one of whom cared a hairpin

for the art of healing; the common object being to
diagnose the wife of the Senior Member of Council,
and to discover in her the skill of an old practitioner.

But, unfortunately, Mrs. Dubersome was not a
better performer at the bedside than she was upon
the boards, and proved to be as clumsy in manipulat-
ing splints and bandages as Mrs. Argus herself.

" No, she has never been a nurse," mused that
lady, " and yet, oh where, oh *where* could I have seen
her before ? "

After these disastrous failures, conjecture regarding Mrs. Dubersome assumed luxuriously fantastic
shapes ; but each theory upon being subjected to the
test which its propounder considered the most certain
for its verification dissolved into thin air in the
crucible, leaving a *caput mortuum* of nescience to
distract the brain of the baffled inquirer.

It having occurred to somebody that he or she had
once seen a face resembling that of Mrs. Dubersome
in a circus-troupe, Mrs. Argus, after long and skilful
manœuvring, succeeded in subjecting that much-
enduring lady to the ordeal of a gallop round the
island ; but as the Councillor's wife swayed about
during the exercise like a bear on a pole, and finished
by assuming a sitting posture on the Mount Road,

it was decided that she had never posed as the rider of six abreast.

Then another ingenious person discovered a likeness between her and a certain provincial concert-singer, but her singing-voice, which, by the way, she was not chary of exercising, disclosed neither natural melody nor culture, and her ignorance of the very rudiments of music blighted the growing hope that she would turn out to have been a governess.

People now began to despair of solving the mystery, but the ladies were unanimous in declaring that whatever Mrs. Dubersome's previous life had been, the lines of it had fallen in places not exactly within the sphere of good society. There was a " something," you know, a " something."

Repulsed at all points, Mrs. Argus was not yet beaten : she was a true Briton in her inability to recognize defeat; and, discomfited in the direct attack, she resolved to adopt the slower but more insidious process of sap and mine.

Acting upon this principle, she exercised her manifold powers of pleasing in endeavouring to gain Mrs. Dubersome's friendship, hoping that when complete intimacy was established that lady might in an

E

unguarded moment impart to her the well-kept
secret of her former life.

To a certain extent Mrs. Argus was successful in
her advances, but she never secured what was her
main object, a footing of familiar friendship; Mrs.
Dubersome, nevertheless, preferred her companionship to that of the other ladies of the place,
and this qualified success was not altogether barren
of result.

One evening as Mrs. Argus was walking on the
beach, she saw her friend and confidante Mrs. Keane
driving by ; whereupon she stopped the carriage, and,
entering it, drove off with her ally.

" A very singular fact has turned up, dear," she
said gravely. " I wonder whether we are all of us
mistaken about that woman. What do you think I
discovered this afternoon ? There was archery going
on at their house, and in shooting I split my bodice
and had to go into her room to be stitched up.
While her maid was away with the dress I examined
the books on the table, and, would you believe it, on
the fly-leaf of every one of them was written ' Lady
Rochester ' ! "

" Very strange," murmured Mrs. Keane, much
interested in this disclosure—" very strange, and yet

Mr. Beauclerk, you remember, told us that her name appears in the Civil Fund records as Blacker. He promised, you know, to go home by Switzerland and find out all about the business there. I think next mail ought to bring me a letter."

"But how does she get the name and title of Lady Rochester?" urged Mrs. Argus.

"Mystery on mystery," sighed Mrs. Keane.

A few days after this conversation the expected communication arrived. Mr. Beauclerk had discovered thus much: The Dubersomes had been married by the British Chaplain at Berne; the lady's name was Blacker, she was a widow, and the witnesses whose signatures were attached to the marriage-register were Lord and Lady Caerlyon.

Mrs. Argus and her friend were now completely baffled, and, being ignorant in what direction to continue their efforts, remained in an attitude of passive expectation, awaiting the revelation which they were sanguine would sooner or later be afforded by time and the chapter of accidents.

At length an event occurred which greatly elevated Mrs. Dubersome in popular estimation and dealt a crushing blow to the phalanx of her traducers.

During the cool season Madras was visited by no less a person than the Duke of Dundee, who had come to India on a shooting excursion. His destination was Nepaul, but as his steamer anchored for a day or two off Madras, he spent the time on shore as a guest at Government House, where a dinner-party was given in his honour.

Among the guests invited to meet him were, as a matter of course, the Dubersomes; and the party, a small and select one, included also Mrs. Keane and Mrs. Argus. The latter lady joined the Dubersomes as they were ascending the large staircase, and promised herself considerable amusement at witnessing Mrs. Dubersome's demeanour when presented to a real live Duke.

Mrs. Keane was already in the room, and as the Dubersomes entered, Mrs. Argus and her ally exchanged a significant smile.

In another moment they stood aghast in speechless amazement, for the Governor's illustrious guest, breaking away from His Excellency, with whom he had till then been engaged in earnest dialogue, approached Mrs. Dubersome, with a cordial smile and outstretched hand, exclaiming joyfully, "Is it really *you!* How glad I am to meet you again.

Tell me, what has brought you to such a distant quarter of the globe?"

"Let me introduce your Grace to my husband, Mr. Dubersome, of the Madras Civil Service," said the lady, courtesying not ungracefully.

The Duke extended his hand to Mr. Dubersome, who bowed in silence.

During this little scene Mrs. Argus, with dilating eyes and straining ears, had stood close behind Mrs. Dubersome.

"And how are the Caerlyons?" continued the Duke.

"I have not seen either Lord or Lady Caerlyon since my marriage, your Grace; I came to India for my honeymoon, and have remained here ever since," replied the Councillor's wife, who seemed quite at her ease with her ducal friend.

"And your pretty yacht? I heard of the mishap. Was it a total wreck?"

"Yes, it was completely broken up, and the timbers were sold at Genoa for a mere song."

"Well, we passed some delightful days in her; the Duchess and Lady Kitty will never forget your kindness to them at Palermo."

Shortly afterwards, dinner was announced, and as

the Governor was living *en garçon*, Mrs. Dubersome, at His Grace's particular request, was taken in to dinner by the Duke. During the long banquet, Mrs. Argus sat as if in a dream ; she ate and drank mechanically, and spoke like an automaton to the unfortunate man to whom she had been assigned as a messmate. Her attention was concentrated upon the Duke and Mrs. Dubersome ; and once she saw the latter actually touch His Grace's arm with her fan. The sight froze her very blood, and nearly gave Mrs. Keane a fit.

If Mrs. Dubersome had lived among peers of the realm from her girlhood, she could not have displayed more *aplomb*, and, what was worse, the Duke was evidently delighted with her. Their conversation never flagged for an instant, and, as the dinner proceeded and the champagne imparted its generous vigour to the lady's spirits, His Grace became more and more entertained by her remarks, and his laughter at her sallies, the purport of which Mrs. Argus sat too far off to catch, was loud and frequent. He sat with his friend during the rest of the evening, and very nearly persuaded her to sing a comic song, but a look from Mr. Dubersome restrained her.

Few women have ever achieved a more complete

social triumph than was enjoyed that evening by
Mrs. Dubersome. After a long period of passive
resistance, the lioness had turned upon her foes.
She had torn Detraction into shreds, had struck
Malice to the earth, and had vindicated her title
to range over the high places.

Henceforward Mrs. Dubersome's position remained
unchallenged. Her secret was still in her own keeping, and appeared likely to remain so. New topics
arose to distract the attention of her censors, and a
well-considered course of hospitality upon which she
now embarked had the effect of rendering her to
a certain extent even popular. Speaking generally,
no one who had come to know Mrs. Dubersome
disliked her. She was good-natured, jovial, and
withal modest. She never posed as the great lady,
though all her actions showed that she possessed a
due sense of what her position required of her in the
direction of generosity and hard work ; and then,
had she not hob-nobbed in the face of men and
angels with a Duke, and had she not conferred
obligations upon a Duke's wife and daughter ?

Once, indeed, Mrs. Argus was on the verge of the
great discovery. The occasion in question was a
large musical party at the Commander-in-Chief's, to

which all the fashionable world had been invited. Among the guests was Captain Manly, the commander of one of the last-launched steamers of the P. and O. fleet. Mrs. Argus, an old friend of the Captain's, was in the act of accepting his invitation to join a party to inspect the vessel on the following morning, when she observed a curious smile stealing over the sailor's weather-beaten face, and following the direction of his eyes she saw that they were fixed upon Mrs. Dubersome, who, with her husband, was at that moment entering the room.

" Do you know Mrs. Dubersome ? " inquired Mrs. Argus eagerly.

" Is that Mrs. Dubersome who is now speaking to Lady—— ? " asked her companion.

" Yes, the lady in black and gold. She is Mrs. Dubersome. Do you know her ? "

" I certainly do not know her under *that* name, and perhaps I may be mistaken in thinking that I know her at all. Would you mind introducing me, I have a sort of idea that we have met before."

The heart of Mrs. Argus beat like that of a panther which has crept within springing distance of a kid. " I shall be only too delighted," said she with alacrity ; and taking the mariner's arm, she

piloted him dexterously through the crowd to the top
of the room, where Mrs. Dubersome had taken her
place by the side of the hostess.

" Don't mention my present ship," whispered the
Captain, " just say of the *Renown.*" Mrs. Argus
nodded.

" Mrs. Dubersome, may I introduce a friend of
mine to you ? " she said, with the sweetness of sugar
of lead, and the gentleness of a vampire—" Captain
Manly, of the *Renown.*"

The effect was electrical. It surprised even Mrs.
Argus, and the charitable soul, with a generous
regard for the happiness of others, looked anxiously
round the room for her friend, Mrs. Keane, in the
hope that she also might witness and enjoy what
was coming.

Mrs. Dubersome's merry brown face blanched; she
rose with a slight tremor, and doubtfully extending
a lifeless hand to the Captain, murmured, what every
line of her countenance belied, that she was very
glad indeed to meet him again, and then, as though
her feet refused their support, she sank with a faint
smile back into a chair.

The music now commenced, and effectually
prevented any further conversation. Captain Manly

and Mrs. Argus—the latter tingling from head to foot with pleasurable excitement—sought a seat at a sufficient distance from the piano to enable them to hear each other's voices. No sooner were they seated than the lady began—

"Now, you must tell me *all* you know about her. In the first place, who was she?"

"You don't mean to say you don't know that?" asked the Captain, smiling at Mrs. Argus's anxiety.

"No; *nobody* knows it," she replied.

"And how long has she been here?" he inquired.

"Oh, more than a year, and as yet we know absolutely *nothing* about her. Now, do, like a dear good man, clear up the mystery."

The Captain paused, and looked at her animated face.

"What are they playing?" he asked, his ear detecting a familiar air.

"*Il Segreto*," replied the lady.

"Most appropriate—can you keep one?"

"Oh, yes," she replied, her eyes sparkling with the light of coming triumph, and she brought her face so close to his that the feather in her bonnet tickled his nose.

"So can I, Mrs. Argus," said the worthy tar, rising and looking at his watch. "Time for me to be on board—good-bye till to-morrow!" and with a careless nod he turned away and left the room.

So the victory remained with the wife of the Senior Member until the time arrived for John Dubersome to retire.

Then addresses began to pour in upon that eminent administrator, and for several days the city was in the throes of farewell entertainments.

A handsome necklace was presented to Mrs. Dubersome by the native merchants in consideration of some trade franchise which had been secured to them by John's exertions; but Mrs. Dubersome, to her honour be it stated, refused the glittering toy, saying that the only person from whom she could receive a gift was her husband.

The Press was loud in the praise of her manifold good works. She was spoken of as one who, by the powerful authority of her position and the generous influence of her purse, had afforded encouragement and support to every charitable institution in the town.

The honours which were showered upon the Dubersomes had such a prejudicial effect upon the

nerves of Mrs. Argus, that, before the week of festival
had closed, that kindly lady was confined to her bed
by an attack of jaundice, and while she lay propped
by pillows and wrapped in shawls, reading the last
and most flattering of the daily panegyrics upon
her enemy, she heard the cannon booming from the
fort, announcing to four-hundred-thousand people
that Martha Dubersome was leaving India for ever.
For ever ! and the great mystery remained unsolved.
The wily foe had triumphed over the best considered
and most ably conducted strategy, and was departing
in the odour of popularity and renown.

As she uttered the last word she thought of Captain
Manly, and how near she had once been to the discovery of the great secret, and with a feeling of
complete prostration, the unhappy woman buried her
yellow face in her pillows and wept the bitter tears
that spring from the Marah of foiled malignity.

*   *   *   *

As soon as Mrs. Argus was sufficiently recovered
to render her removal advisable, her doctor sent
her to England.

During the voyage she spent most of the time in
her cabin, speaking to no one but the ship's

surgeon, and wearing the appearance of one upon whose life a scathing blight had fallen.

On the day preceding the ship's arrival at London she came on deck for the first time, and passed an hour sitting under the lee of the skylight languidly conversing with the chief officer.

An outward-bound vessel as it passed them dipped her flag. "That's my old ship," said the sailor, scanning her through his telescope, "the old *Renown*. It's high time she was taken off the line." The *Renown !* Captain Manly's old ship !—At the name of this vessel, Mrs. Argus began for the first time to display some interest in her companion's remarks.

"By the way," he continued, "did you ever come across a Mrs. Dubersome in your Presidency ?"

"Mrs. Dubersome !" almost shrieked the lady. "Yes, I am very well acquainted with her. When— where—what do you know about her ?"

"Lucky woman, wasn't she?" remarked the young man, still regarding the vessel through his glass.

"Lucky ! How was she lucky ?" gasped Mrs. Argus, whose instinct assured her that now at last she stood upon the threshold of revelation.

"Didn't she marry a Member of Council, or some

one of that sort ? " inquired her companion, closing
his telescope and looking at Mrs. Argus.

" Yes, yes," panted the invalid—" go on."

" Thousands a year, they get, don't they? "—
Mrs. Argus gave a confirmatory moan.—" And a
thousand a year pension ? " continued the sailor.

" Widows get only three hundred," quavered the
lady—" but do, *do* go on."

" And isn't that pretty well for a stewardess? "

" A stewardess ! " ejaculated Mrs. Argus, with
flaming eyes.

" Yes, she was for three years stewardess on board
the *Renown*, and left it for the *Lady Rochester*, Lord
Caerlyon's yacht. The Caerlyons took such a fancy
to her that they treated her more like a relative
than a dependant, and I believe it was when they
were all going home across the Continent, after their
yacht had been wrecked by a levanter, that she met
Mr. Dubersome. Mrs. Argus, you seem to be very
ill ? "

" Take me below," sighed Mrs. Argus; " I am
fainting."

A NIGHT IN AN OLD FORT.

At the close of the year 186— my work led me into the wildest part of a district celebrated in Indian annals for the stubborn contest waged in former days by its local chiefs against the best Generals of Aurungzebe, a resistance which, though in the end overpowered by the superior resources of the Imperial power, secured to the population a longer period of immunity from Mohammedan exaction than was enjoyed by any of the neighbouring provinces.

On the evening of the 15th of November—this date, as will afterwards be seen, has an interesting significance—at the close of a long and wearisome march, I reached a little village where I had made arrangements to halt for the night.

I found, however, that my tent had not arrived, and that my servants had placed the bed and other component parts of my modest equipage under a moss-covered stone archway that once formed one of the gateways of a formidable Rajput stronghold, long since deserted, and now in ruins.

The gateway, which had been well swept out, afforded complete shelter from both wind and rain ; and, as there was no other accommodation available, I thankfully accepted the situation.

As the sun had not quite set, I took advantage of what daylight still remained, to stroll along the ruined rampart in company with an intelligent old villager, who, as he claimed descent from the last of the Killedars, or fort commandants, I hoped might be able to afford some information throwing light upon the history of what had evidently been in former days an important place of arms.

As we wandered among the fallen stones, half-hidden by sand-binder and ground-ivy, my guide pointed out the ruins of the various watch-towers which, placed upon a higher elevation than the rest of the fortifications, stood out sharp and sombre against the sky.

That distant one was called the Tara-Brûj ; this, the Miriam Brûj ; the one over there, the Sultan Brûj—appellations which, from their etymology, had clearly no earlier date than the period when the place came into the possession of the Moghuls.

We were standing upon the rampart that crowned the old gateway within which I was to pass the night ; and, as I looked at the massive walls, now a prey to that vegetation which in the East destroys neglected masonry as surely as rust corrodes iron, I thought of the line of the Persian poet—"The spider and the owl reign in the halls of Afrasiab."

My companion could not tell me much regarding the early history of the place. There had been wars, frequent and severe, but in the end the Mohammedans had triumphed. Then came the English, and the power of the Crescent had waned. His grandfather had been the last of the Killedars—he knew no more.

Returning to my impromptu chamber I ate my simple camp dinner, and after smoking a cheroot or two went to bed. I was tired out, and was soon in the land of dreams.

I might have slept for an hour, when I became aware of the pressure of a hand that was placed firmly, but not roughly, upon my shoulder.

Starting up, I saw standing by my side a European dressed in the garb of a soldier as one sees it depicted in prints illustrating Indian military life in the early part of the last century. His face, which was of the most resolute type, wore an air of

F

extreme anxiety, and though his manner was grave
and deliberate, he gave me the idea of one who was
conscious of some serious and immediate danger.

"Get up," he said to me. "Get up, sir, I want
this gear," pointing to my scanty furniture, "foot-
sacked at once."

Seeing that I hesitated, he explained, "I want
fair play for the guns."

"Guns!" I ejaculated, "what on earth are you
talking about?"

"There will be hot work in this gateway pre-
sently," was the reply; "I have warned them inside,
but warn as you may, it's no use. Now the old chief's
dead, they let things take their chance. Come," he resumed, with some asperity, "you had better get out
of this archway if you think your life worth saving."

"Where shall I go?" I asked, utterly bewildered
as my eye fell upon some strange-looking natives,
who were busily closing and fastening an immense
gate, which till then I had not observed.

"Follow me," said the soldier, and, turning on his
heel, he led the way into the precincts of the fort.

He first ascended the rampart upon which I had
stood the previous evening. The night was dark,
save for the light afforded by the stars, but I could

see that the place had undergone a complete change; there were now no loose stones to impede one's progress; the parapet, no longer crumbling and uneven, now stood as high as a man's breast, and was furnished with a revetment of freshly hewn stone. Lights were twinkling from the various watch-turrets ; the Sultan Brûj was brilliantly illuminated, and from that direction came now and again faint strains of festive music.

My companion, with a disdainful jerk of the hand, said bitterly, "Still sitting at the nautch, though I told them four hours ago we should be attacked to-night. Why, sir, as I rode this evening by the banks of the river, I saw the whole Moghul army encamped this side of the ford. There they come!" he exclaimed, pointing to a large dark moving mass which his practised eye readily recognized to be marching men, "and they are moving straight upon this gateway, the only weak point in the whole fort. What's this!" he continued—a rope hung over the crest of the wall with a lantern at the end of it—"There's *treachery* here," he muttered, as he hauled up the tell-tale lamp; "they have got the direction now, and, at the rate they are marching, five minutes brings them to the gate, so we'll go down."

We accordingly descended, and my companion led me to a small bastion, which had been hastily thrown up in a re-entering angle of the inner rampart. In the little fieldwork stood two quaint-looking Indian cannons, carefully trained upon the archway.

" Grape and canister," grimly remarked the soldier pointing to the battery round which were clustered some dozen native soldiers dressed and armed in the picturesque irregularity of a bygone age. Behind them stood, grim and silent, a line of about a score of musqueteers.

"Prime and load," was the low command. The musqueteers had evidently been well trained, and the order was obeyed with swift precision.

By the side of each gun stood a native cannonier, upright and motionless, holding in his hand a burning linstock, the dancing flame of which, as it lighted up the warlike groups and the fantastic guns with their dragon-shaped heads, formed a picture which might have glowed from the canvas of Salvator Rosa.

The oppression of the solemn silence that ensued was unendurable. My nerves were strained to the utmost pitch of tension and I panted for the catastrophe. Suddenly I became aware of a faint sound which might have been the wind in the trees outside, but which, to my anxious ear, fully prepared for what was coming, appeared to be the distant, though rapidly approaching tramp of men. As I listened, it gradually developed into the subdued murmur of a mighty host advancing with the utmost caution. All at once the sound was hushed; the mute battalions were at the walls; but as yet on neither side had a shot been fired, or a word spoken.

I glanced at the soldier, wondering what his next act would be; he was leaning forward, listening intently, his left hand grasped a spoke of the gun-wheel, while his right held an old-fashioned flint carabine; a slight breeze that had sprung up played with a grizzled curl upon his bronzed forehead and stirred the lappets of his coat; but for this he might have been a figure cut in stone.

Ever and anon, from the Sultan Brûj, there came borne upon the wind the faint sound of the dholki and the sitar, announcing that the young chiefs were still at their revels; but saving these whispering cadences the fort was voiceless as the citadel of Tadmor.

The torturing stillness was at length broken by a stealthy footstep. Some one was descending the ramp leading from the top of the gate. In a few seconds I discerned a man carrying a flambeau; he took the direction of the gate, and as he passed the battery the light of the torch fell full upon his face ; it was that of a Brahmin ; craft, eagerness, and fear seemed to blend in its expression ; in his hand he held a large key, but as his trembling fingers inserted it in the lock of the gate, a shot from the soldier's firelock rang out through the silence of the night, and the traitor, leaving the key still pressing upon the unturned wards, fell dead against the threshold.

The report of the musket was the signal for a perfect hurricane of sound without. Kettle-drums struck up, trumpets brayed, words of command were uttered, and soon the roar of a field-piece reverberated through the archway ; the shot hurtled through the wooden door, ricochetted over our little battery, and buried itself in some remote quarter of the fort.

" That ought to waken them," laughed the soldier savagely. " There goes the gate," he cried, as the discharge of several guns together hurled the obstruction into the arch, and strewed the floor with blazing splinters and smouldering beams.

Our men, who were now crouching behind the parapet, received no injury. I had stooped for safety with the rest—the soldier alone stood erect. " If I can only hold my own here till those curs get under arms!'" he growled, as he looked anxiously behind him for some sign of approaching succour.

The Moghul kettle-drums now beat the advance, and a crowd of men surged headlong into the gateway; they were led by a tall warrior, whose chain-mail coat and bright steel cap flashed in the light of the burning timbers.

" By single guns from the right—Fire!" shouted the soldier.

A torrent of flame poured from the right-hand gun; and the archway, which a moment before had been thronged with living men, was now heaped with dead and writhing bodies.

Then, thank Heaven! we could hear the sound of drums and horns, shouts of command and cries of warning in the interior of the fort, which told us that the garrison was afoot: but would the reinforcement be in time to save the gate?

Once more the kettle-drums of the assailants sounded the onslaught, and again the stormers rushed forward, uttering mad yells of " *Deen*."* When they had penetrated half-way through the arch, the soldier gave the order to fire the second gun; the linstock

---

* The faith.

was applied to the vent, but the only response was a flash of priming—the dragon-mouth was mute.

The soldier hurriedly bent over the breech. " Spiked ! " he groaned between his set teeth, " spiked by that infernal Brahmin ! "

The enemy's advance had in the meantime been checked for the moment by a well-aimed volley from our musqueteers, whose fire, delivered at less than quarter point-blank range, swept through that closely packed multitude with the effect of a scythe upon meadow grass.

Seeing that the musqueteers were now engaged in re-charging their pieces, and that the right-hand gun was still unloaded, though the cannoniers were busy at their work, the soldier drew his sabre, and, calling to the nearest men to follow him, dashed into the gateway, which was rapidly filling with shields and tulwars preparatory to a fresh irruption.

I could now see lights flitting about in all directions in the interior of the fort, and could also hear the sound of men, though still at a distance, hastening towards the gate.

In the meantime the soldier and the dozen or two sipahis who had followed him were hard at work with cut, guard, point, and parry in the archway.

The Indians were soon all beaten down, yet the Englishman, by dint of a splendid courage, and what appeared to me to be superhuman strength and activity, for a few precious moments held his own. Man after man fell beneath his powerful strokes, but the enemy, continually reinforced from without, and pushed forward by weight of numbers, steadily pressed him back. " Gun got ready," cried the men at the fieldpiece, in their quaint rendering of the English which they had learnt from their commander.

Had the soldier turned at this juncture, the stormers would have entered the place with him, and the fort would have fallen: it was thus necessary at all hazards to hold the gateway till support arrived.

The gallant fellow fully grasped the situation : he saw the sacrifice that was demanded, and his noble soul decreed that the gate should be held yet a few moments longer, though he bought the respite by his own annihilation. Raising his voice till it resounded clear and strong above the din of battle, he thundered forth his last command—" FIRE ! "

The gunner hesitated for an instant, then the flaming match fell upon the priming, and the roar of the cannon was the soldier's requiem.

Once more the gate was swept clear of the enemy, and ere the echoes of the discharge had well died away, I heard shouts and the tramp of men advancing to our rescue at the double. Before the Mussulmans could gather head for a third assault, our men had filled up the gateway with great stones and sandbags, of which a large number had previously been collected near the spot, but by a procrastination that had nearly proved fatal, had been allowed to remain as a refuge for rats and squirrels. The walls were rapidly manned, and a brisk fire was opened from the numerous jezails and other pieces that lined them. The attempt at a surprise had failed, and the Imperial army, after much uproar and a vast expenditure of powder, slowly retreated.

*   *   *   *

I turned in my bed, stretched myself, and awoke. The sunlight was streaming between the stonework of the arch and the massive side-posts, from which in former days a gate had been suspended. The sound of the lascar's mallet outside told me that my tardy tent was being pitched, and as I drank the cup of tea which my servant handed to me, I resolved to commit my dream to writing.

Some years afterwards an opportunity presented

itself of consulting an old history of the district, and turning to the account given of the fort, I read with much interest the following statement :—

" The importance of this ancient stronghold lay mainly in its position, which, commanding the chief ford of the river, enabled its possessors during a long series of years to oppose a successful resistance to the encroachments of the Moghuls. Not the least among the many formidable perils through which this fortress passed unscathed was a skilfully-planned surprise on the night of the 15th November, 1670. The attempt was conducted by the redoubtable Lushkar Khan, the most enterprising of the Imperial Generals, but the assault, though of a determined nature, and assisted by treachery from within, was frustrated by an act of sublime devotion on the part of an Englishman, a deserter from the Hon'ble Company's Army. This man had been condemned to death for some military offence, but contriving to escape on the very morning appointed for his execution, had succeeded in gaining the territory of —— with whose Chief he took service. The full details of the act by which he saved the fort are now unknown."

THE JUNGLE FEE.

"Why do you call your house 'The Fee?'" I inquired of my old friend, Dr. Mactaggart, as we sat after dinner in the snug smoking-room of his little shooting-box in Fifeshire.

The Doctor cleared his throat. The whisky-toddy and the fragrant honeydew were shedding their genial influence over both of us. He was in the mood for story-telling, and I was in the right frame of mind to listen.

"It came about in this manner," he said. "When I was an army surgeon in India, medical men were not so plentiful out there as they are now, and we were moved from place to place as the necessity for our services arose. It was during these frequent marches that I made my natural history collection that you were admiring this afternoon; for, whenever time permitted, I never lost an opportunity of leaving the high road for a day or two, and making a *détour*

through a likely-looking bit of jungle or an un-
frequented range of mountains.

" In the summer of 185— I was suddenly ordered
from Masulipatam, on the Coromandel Coast, to
Secunderabad, in the Deccan.   I was well aware of
the sort of country that I should have to pass through,
and knowing that very rapid travelling could not
be expected from me during that sultry season, I
got ready my rifle and fowling-piece.

" I determined to strike off the road for a few
marches in an endeavour to gain some rocks near
the Kistna river, my object being to secure a specimen of the small dog-leopard, which I had heard
was to be found there.   I made my digression, but
did not bag my leopard, and, in trying to get back
to the main road, I lost my way.   I was travelling
with all my baggage, no great amount in those
days, and had with me a small tent, which always
accompanied me on my excursions; and as my
coolies were carrying a supply of food for three
days, there was nothing to occasion any great
anxiety in being lost for twenty-four hours or so.

" I had marched without a halt from sunrise till
four o'clock in the afternoon, when a sudden turn
of the jungle-track brought me upon the very last

thing that I had expected to see in those wilds—a theodolite. A man dressed like a second-rate sort of European was bending over it. He raised his head with a smothered execration as he heard us approaching, and stared at me defiantly.

"He was a gaunt, bony man of about five-and-forty, with a good deal of strength in his tall, loosely-knit frame. His face was a peculiar one—half tiger, half cobra. I had more than once observed the type when I was in medical charge of the European goal at Ooty, and by certain laws of association, too subtle to analyse, the idea produced by it in my mind was connected with coldly calculated murder, carefully planned and pitilessly carried out. The expression which this forbidding countenance assumed at my sudden appearance seemed to convey: 'What the deuce do you mean by trespassing in *my* jungle? *I'm* master here.'

"I wished him good day, and, in a friendly manner, inquired how I should proceed in order to strike the high road between two stages, the names of which I had gathered from my route-book.

"He stared at me insolently for a moment, and then in a strong Tipperary brogue told me to go straight on for a quarter of a mile, when I should come to where the pathway branched to the right and left. I was on no account to turn to the left, as it would lead me, he said, ' the divil knows where,' but the right-hand turn would bring me in less than half an hour to the high road. On reaching the turning, I observed two natives approaching from the left; one of them was carrying a basket, which I concluded belonged to the man from whom I had just parted. As they were coming from the direction which I had been so especially cautioned to avoid, I stopped, and, questioning them as to my route, was much surprised to hear that I was within ten minutes' walk of the high road, which lay in the direction from which they had just come. The right-hand track, they said, ran to a deserted village lying in the very heart of the jungle. ' Plenty tiger there,' they added, with a grin.

"Conceiving that the European's directions arose from a mistake—since he could have no object in sending me so far adrift from my course—I followed the instructions of the coolies, and in a short time, to my great relief, for the sun was already sinking, I emerged from the wilderness into an open space shaded by a few lofty trees, under which stood three tents of different sizes.

"This little encampment I discovered belonged to my friend of the theodolite; I therefore determined to pitch my own modest bit of canvas at a sufficient distance from his belongings to make us at any rate not quite next-door neighbours; and as I proposed to continue my journey early on the following morning, I did not expect to see his ugly face again.

"While I was superintending the pitching of my *be-choba** a servant came from one of the stranger's tents, and, after exchanging a few words with one of my people, approached me with a polite salaam, and saying that he had just learnt that I was a Doctor Sahib, begged that I would come over and see his mistress, who, he said, looking at me earnestly, was 'Very bad sick.' She had been taken ill shortly after her husband went out in the morning, and although word of her condition had twice been sent to him, he had treated the report as exaggerated, and, saying that he was engaged on some very important work, had refused to come back.

"On entering the tent, I saw a homely-featured, middle-aged woman lying on a bed; she was completely dressed, and had evidently been surprised by

---

* Tent without a pole.

the attack while engaged in her ordinary duties, for a piece of needlework lay beside her, and her thimble was still on her finger.

" I examined her very carefully, and, from the symptoms displayed, I came to the conclusion that she was under the influence of some powerful irritant poison.

" Her account of the seizure was that she had lately been suffering from intermittent fever of the ordinary Indian type, that her husband, before going out that morning, had given her some medicine which he had prepared himself, and that shortly after taking it she had become alarmingly ill.

" I asked her if she had any of the medicine left. The bottle was standing on a little table close by, and was nearly full. Putting my tongue to the cork I was at once aware of a strong bitter taste resembling that of arsenic, and knowing that this poison was sometimes administered in small quantities in cases of fever, I suspected that she was suffering from an overdose.

" In reply to my inquiry as to where her husband kept his medicines, she pointed to a large box in a corner of the tent, in which she said I should find a small medicine-chest.

" I opened the large box and extracted the little chest from under a heap of clothes; but was unable to examine it, as it was locked, and the man had the key.

" I gave my patient some calcined magnesia, and set to work to analyse the solution, to which I applied Reinsch's test, and there were the octahedral crystals of arsenious acid as plain, my dear fellow, as the sugar in this tumbler.

" I then treated the woman regularly for arsenical poisoning, and having a suspicion of possible foul play I took the liberty of impounding the little medicine-chest ; being determined to see the contents of it, come what might.

" By the time of her husband's return, which was very late, my patient was out of danger ; and as I heard the man's harsh voice giving orders outside the tent, I whispered to her not to take any more medicine from him, but to proceed at once to the nearest station and seek medical advice. She replied by a grateful look of intelligence.

"'Hulloa, what are ye doin' in my tint, misther?' The fellow had entered the tent and was evidently startled to see me there.

" ' I am treating your wife, who has called me in.'

"'She wants no tratement; the woman has only got

the faver, and you don't inter this tint again unless *I* send for ye. D'ye hear that ? '

" ' May I ask what you have been giving your wife for her fever ? ' I inquired mildly.

" Givin' her ? Why, qui-nine, to be shure. What ilse should I be afther givin' her ? '

" ' Did you give her nothing else but quinine this morning ? ' I asked.

" ' Divil a thing else—why do ye ask ? Who are ye ? Ye're not a docthor ? '

" ' I *am* a doctor, and I am treating your wife, not for fever, but for arsenical poisoning,' I said, looking my man straight in the face.

" He changed colour and glanced round the tent. ' Where's that midsin as I give ye this mornin' ? ' he said, turning abruptly to his wife, who lay trembling and silent during our dialogue.

" I replied for her : ' The medicine is in my possession. I have subjected it to analysis, and have found it to contain sufficient arsenic to kill the three of us.'

" The man with a smothered oath walked to the large box, opened it, and peered in. I knew what was coming, and, bidding the poor woman good-night, hastened over to my tent and slipped a revolver into my pocket

" In another moment the man was in front of me, foaming with rage. ' Where's me black box, ye thafe?' he shouted. ' Where's me midsin box?'

" 'I have it carefully secured among my baggage,' I replied calmly, ' and to-morrow both it and yourself will be in the hands of the police.'

" 'I'll have it out of ye, ye plunderin' villin,' he said, picking up a billet of wood that lay near, and coming towards me with a threatening countenance. I quickly drew my Colt and covered him. I suppose I was getting excited myself, for I said, ' You poisoning rascal, do you think I have not got evidence enough to transport you again?'

" At these words he started, and moved by a sort of inspiration, I added, 'I know you, you're an ex-convict, and I'm the Inspector of Police of this division. You're my prisoner,' and I tapped him on the shoulder in proper regulation form.

" The wretch dropped his stick, and stood glowering upon me with his ghastly face, his eyes staring, and his half-open mouth twitching convulsively. He had not been shaved for three days, and his stubbly chin and upper lip gave him the most utterly scoundrel look I should think it possible for the human face to wear.

"I had, figuratively speaking, floored him, but it was necessary to say something more in order to carry out my *rôle;* I therefore added, 'You will sleep to-night in that tent,' pointing to the most distant of the three, 'and you will approach your wife at your peril. To-morrow I shall take you to B——. Right about face—quick march.'

"He turned as if in a dream, and walked slowly to the little tent. As soon as he had disappeared, I despatched a hurriedly-pencilled letter to the senior police officer at B—— asking him to come well attended to the encampment without delay; and then I went to bed with my revolver under my pillow and the medicine-box by my side.

" Early the following morning Mrs. O'Meara, for that proved to be my patient's name, sent for me. I found her pale and weak, but convalescent. She told me that her husband had ridden off during the night, and she had a presentiment that he would never return, but at the same time she entreated that I would not leave her until I had placed her under the charge of the Inspector of Police.

" Upon that officer's arrival we broke open the medicine-box. It contained phials full of different kinds of poisons, none of which had apparently been used except one holding arsenic, from which a certain amount had been taken.

" While we were conducting this examination one of the constables who had accompanied the Inspector appeared at the tent-door and silently beckoned to him.

" In a few minutes the latter returned, and called me out.

" ' I will show you something, sir,' he said, 'which will throw a very clear light on this case,' and he led me to a thick and tangled brake lying just within the margin of the jungle.

" ' Look here,' he continued, pointing to a freshly-dug hole, long and narrow, and some six feet in depth.

" ' This is a grave !' said I, ' what does it all mean ? ' My companion lifted the adjacent under-growth with his whip, and disclosed a hastily-made coffin.

" ' There is no doubt,' he said, ' for whom these preparations were made, and it is clear that but little time would have elapsed between death and burial.'

The whole hideous affair was now clear to me, and I returned with the officer in silence to the tent.

" In reply to the Inspector's questions, Mrs.

O'Meara told us that she had been married to O'Meara only recently, she had made his acquaintance in Calcutta, where she had for the last few years been living on the interest of a small fortune left to her by a former husband, a shopkeeper there. O'Meara, when she first knew him, was in the Public Works Department, but had afterwards been dismissed for some serious irregularity; he had managed, however, to obtain an appointment under a south-country Zemindar, for whom he was at the present time doing some surveying work. She supposed that O'Meara had married her for her money, and now wished to get rid of her, seeing that he had obliged her to make her will in his favour, and had treated her ever since their marriage with daily increasing cruelty, dragging her about into the most unhealthy localities, presumably in the hope that she would succumb to the climate, the effects of which it was now apparent that he had resolved upon supplementing by the administration of poison.

"The plot had been well laid. Had the woman died, she would have been buried as soon as the breath had left her body, and the victim being the wife of a European, no suspicion would have been aroused. If by chance any rumour of foul play had

got abroad, inquiry in such a wild locality would
have been futile; for during the height of the
summer season in India a very brief period would
suffice to render medical examination in such a
case an impossibility.

"A pursuit was organized, but the rascal made good
his escape. Australia was his point, but he was fated
never to reach it. The ship in which he sailed was
caught in a cyclone in the Bay of Bengal, and in the
height of the tempest O'Meara was washed over-
board.

"Mrs. O'Meara, after her return to Calcutta, more
than once wrote to beg my acceptance of some
valuable present, which I, believing her to be by no
means a rich woman, politely but firmly declined.
Imagine my surprise when, shortly after my retire-
ment from the service, I received a letter from her
lawyer informing me that Mrs. O'Meara had lately
died, leaving me as my fee for services rendered, a
legacy of her entire fortune. The amount was a
little over £5,000, the biggest honorarium that I
ever received or ever heard of; and as it enabled me
to buy this cottage and bit of moor, I thought I
could not do better than call the place after it—the
'Jungle Fee.'"

MR. MAGNUS.

Mr. Lemuel Magnus, C.I.E., was British Resident at the Court of our faithful feudatory, the Rajah of Lilipatam.

During his long tenure of this appointment Mr. Magnus had introduced not a few important reforms into the administration. Before his accession the pre-Hunterian conception of spelling which had obtained for a couple of hundred years or so, still lingered in Court and Cutcherry; and even in official documents it was the custom to write the Rajah's dominions, Leilapatnam; but the new Resident changed all that with a stroke of his pen. He found the Residency servants, in point of number, only very slightly in excess of his actual requirements, and, in the matter of livery, modestly attired in simple raiment of white muslin : within a month they were a legion gleaming in purple and gold, and whenever Mr. Magnus cried, " What ho ! without there ? " or employed the Eastern equivalent of that summons, his order was echoed by a responsive chorus of " My Lord " from a dozen voices.

Under his predecessor, the Resident's hours for the transaction of public business were definite and well known to the profane crowd; but the labours of Mr. Magnus were esoteric : he sagely deemed that a decent veil of mystery should enshroud an Eastern Jupiter while he forged his thunderbolts, and to all intents and purposes a Jupiter he meant to be.

In this determination, however, Jove somewhat exceeded his warrant. A Resident at a native Court is not sent there to govern; but Mr. Magnus held that his mission on earth was to rule his fellow-men, who, in fact, were primarily created for that particular purpose. From his earliest youth, from the days when, having established supreme control over his smaller brethren in the nursery, he ruled unquestioned over sugar-basin and jam-pot, and thus first tasted the sweets of dominion, he had made it the business of his life to subdue and enslave all people more ductile than himself whom chance brought in his way; and he had encountered many such in his Indian career.

His personal appearance was in perfect harmony

with his character: the pompous pose of the globular
waistcoat, the supercilious gleam of the tenacious
eye, the arrogant set of the head, with its great
bulge in the region of self-esteem, and the self-
assertive pitch of the aggressive nose—all unmistak-
ably announced the autocratic bully.

But as every creature in the organized world has
its oppressor, so there was one human being of whom
our autocrat stood in perpetual awe.

He lived in wholesome terror of his wife; who, it
may be observed, was, at the period of which we
write, superintending the education of sundry minor
Magnuses in England.

The Rajah was a meek young man, devoted to
peace and pleasure, and so long as the indulgence of
his own personal gratifications was not interfered
with, he was only too willing to give the Resident a
free hand in the management of whatever matters of
State that masterful person might take a fancy to
control. This, it is needless to say, was a disposition
that exactly suited the Resident, and the Rajah was
always described by him as an "enlightened ruler."

One morning after breakfast while Mr. Magnus
was in his study, smoking a capital Havannah and
reading a questionable French novel, a resplendent

peon brought in a card on a silver salver, which, like everything engravable in the Residency, bore the Magnus crest, namely, a peacock *or*, with tail expanded.

On the card, traced with a bad quill pen, was the name :—

" Mr. De Lacey Sneape."

The potentate glanced at the modest piece of pasteboard with a fine scorn upon his haughty nose. " Sneape—Sneape—Sneape !—no such name in the service—no such name in the Presidency. Some loafer ! " he muttered to himself. " Let him wait," he growled with his eyes still upon the book, as he arranged himself in a more comfortable attitude.

After about half-an-hour Mr. Magnus, having finished his cigar, rang a little silver bell. The gorgeous attendant re-entered.

" Tell Mr.—ah—," glancing at the card, " Sneape, that he can come in," and seating himself at an enormous table, the Resident opened a volume of Government Orders that happened to be near, and scattering a number of old documents in front of him, began to write upon a large sheet of foolscap with an air of the severest concentration.

The peon returned, but Mr. Magnus, though he knew that some one was in the room, did not look up. This was his favourite manner of receiving unvalued visitors.

After two or three minutes of this show of self-abandonment to toil he raised his head.

" The gentleman has gone," said the peon.

" Gone! " shouted the Resident, throwing down his pen.

" He said, O nourisher of the poor! that he was staying in the public bungalow."

The Pro-Prætor rose, and lighting a fresh cigar, retired with Zola into the ease of a long arm-chair.

An hour or two later, old Parusaram, the palace Dewan, craved the honour of five minutes' interview with the Resident; and after inquiring with much respectful solicitude after that gentleman's health, proceeded to advert to the object of his visit.

" One Sneape Saib, a merchant, has arrived in this place. Has he paid his respects to your Honour ? "

Mr. Magnus, with a pompous wave of the hand towards the card on the table, intimated that the stranger had not been oblivious of that sacred duty.

" He called upon *me* yesterday," continued the

Dewan, looking narrowly at the Resident's broad face, endeavouring to discover whether the visitor had found favour in the eyes of the great man, "asking about a grant of land, and the concession of certain privileges with regard to a rhea-mill that he wants to establish in this place."

In Lilipatam the leading product of the soil is rhea grass, by means of which men of optimistic tendencies have been heard to foretell for the Lilipatians wealth beyond the dreams even of Eastern avarice. But Mr. Magnus pronounced such views to be the twaddle of the visionary, or the ranting of the rogue; so the rhea waved in futile luxuriance over plains that never yielded the State a cowrie-shell of revenue.

"And what answer, pray, did you give to Mr. Sncape?" inquired the great man, knitting his brows ominously.

"I referred him to your Honour's lordship. What power had *I* to give him any answer?" replied the Brahmin, who had long ago taken the measure of Mr. Magnus' heavy foot.

The Resident glared majestic approval. "Who is this person?" he asked.

"I gathered from his conversation, sir, that he

was in some way connected with a firm of merchants in Liverpool."

"Ah! a *Bagman:* I thought so. Well, Dewan, you will tell Mr. De Lacey Sneape," said Mr. Magnus, in his most offensively autocratic manner, "that His Highness declines, peremptorily declines, to concede him either land or privileges; and mind that you say it in such a manner that he will understand it to be conclusive. It is no use his applying to me. You can now take your leave."

The Dewan arose, and, respectfully placing two small limes on the table, salaamed devoutly, and withdrew; but as he left the room he thus inwardly apostrophized the Resident: "O son of an ass! O pig! how I should rejoice to beat your pompous mouth with my oldest and dirtiest slipper!"

"We don't want any factories here," soliloquized Mr. Magnus, " poisoning the air with their filthy smoke, spoiling the view with their ugly chimneys, and rousing me in the morning with their infernal whistle. I had enough of that when I was a boy."

Lemuel Magnus was of humble origin, and had been born and bred in a factory town, where he would have gravitated to some mill as clerk or accountant, had not a distant relative taken him by the hand, and, finding that the youth possessed powers of application and a good memory, ran him with success for the Indian Civil Service.

Why so much about a single character in such a short story ? Dear reader, you don't know Mr. Magnus; he takes the lion's share of everything. I could not epitomize him after the manner of the Dewan.

The European community of Lilipatam had been bidden to a large dinner to be given that evening at the Residency; and it occurred to Mr. Magnus that he would invite also Mr. Sneape, so that the stranger might be impressed with the might and majesty of an Indian Resident, and, returning to Liverpool, recount to wondering and envious colleagues how royally he had been entertained by Mr. Lemuel Magnus, C.S. and C.I.E.

As he drove his high-stepping roans that afternoon past the public bungalow, Mr. Magnus saw an elderly man seated in the verandah reading a book. That, then, must be Mr. Sneape; so, dashing into the compound with a prance and a clatter, the Resident pulled up his champing coursers with the flourish of an Imperial charioteer, and shouted harshly for the attendant, who, hastily tying his turban the while, came running breathlessly from some outlying quarter.

"Deliver this card to Mr. Sneape," commanded the Resident, as he put his horses again in motion. The domestic handed the card to the gentleman with the book, who read the august words:—

"Mr. Lemuel Magnus, C.S., C.I.E.,
"Resident at Lilipatam;"

and on the reverse he deciphered a few lines scrawled in pencil inviting him to dinner at eight o'clock that evening.

The stranger played musingly with the card for a few moments and then put it in his pocket.

"I will go," he said to himself, "anything is better than this dreary hovel."

The dinner was what is called a "*burra khana.*" In plain English, everything was exuberant, heavy, and slow.

The guest from the bungalow was the last to arrive, and the host, coldly giving him the tips of his fingers, turned away, and in an audible tone directed the butler, who was lurking in the doorway, to bring dinner immediately.

During the interval that elapsed between the order

and the announcement, the stranger found himself among some dozen or fifteen people, all of whom were too much engaged in talking among themselves to bestow any attention upon him. The position was an uncomfortable one, and Mr. Magnus intended that it should be so.

When dinner was announced the guests trooped into the room in recognized order, for in Lilipatam precedence was studied as a fine art, and Mr. Sneape found himself, unfriended and solitary, slowly bringing up the rear.

As the party could have filled the table without him, he was placed at one of the corners, where he was forced to rely for conversation upon an old lady who was deaf, and a young man who was patronizing. Thus, long before the dismal dinner had dragged itself through its appointed courses, he sighed for a cup of tea and the slippered ease of the bungalow; thinking that even a damp cheroot among the snakes in the compound would be preferable to this.

At last the ladies rose to leave the room, and the gentlemen, clutching their napkins and the backs of their chairs, smirked benignly and rearranged themselves. The patronizing young gentleman, who was the Resident's assistant, now moved into the august neighbourhood of his chief, in order to receive enlightenment touching certain leading topics of the day upon which that eminent man was pronouncing judgment. Although the stranger, now more isolated than ever, was, owing to local circumstances, excluded from the conversation, he enjoyed on the other hand enlarged opportunities of improving his mind as a listener. He heard much that surprised him, but he marvelled most to observe that at the table of this high Indian official everything relating to Indian matters was carefully eschewed, and that the most favoured subjects of discourse were European politics, scandal in high life at home, and English racing; these, with a little mild dilettantism, presented matter of wider interest to the Resident than did the squalid topics of local life.

"Mr.—ah, Sneape, will you have any more wine? No? Then we will join the ladies," said Mr. Magnus, rising from his chair; and the person addressed inwardly thanked him for not further prolonging the purgatorial repast.

On the following morning the stranger left for England. In the afternoon the English mail arrived

at Lilipatam; it brought the usual weekly letter
from Mrs. Magnus, from which we extract the
following :—" I find it *most* difficult to get into
society in this place.   The county families form
a clique into which there appears to be *no* admission,
but a chance has just presented itself which I
do hope and trust you will not allow to slip.
The Lord Lieutenant, Lord Tymberdale, of Delacey
Court, the finest place in the West, has gone to
India, *incog.*, in order to see and hear for himself
all the ins and outs of trade and administration,
and so forth.   I have only just heard that he includes
Lilipatam in his tour.   Now, Lemuel, you will
of course show him all the attention in your power,
and make a friend of him—it will be of incalculable
service to us in the future.   His *nom de voyage* is
De Lacey Sneape."

THE RISHI AND THE SACRED DIAMOND.

THE following story was told me by my friend Jack
Danby, a gentleman-inspector of police on the
Madras establishment :—

Shortly after I joined the Police department, I
was posted to one of the Telugu districts. My head-
quarters were in a small town called Suugamkondah,
which stood at the foot of a great rocky hill not far
from the meeting place of the Mudiair and Isuka
rivers.

The junction of these streams, forming what is
called a *sungam*, of course rendered the neighbourhood remarkably holy ; and the town, which was full
of Brahmins, contained a flourishing temple to
Akasáramana.

The temple formed, from a police point of view, the
most important feature of the place; for the idol was
incrusted with precious stones, and wore in the centre
of its forehead an enormous diamond presented in

bygone ages by a pious Rajah ; the gem was said to be worth several lakhs of rupees.

This shrine was the most prominent difficulty that lay before me. Although the premises were most carefully guarded, it was plain that a thief had access to the sanctuary. Fourteen months before I assumed charge of the division, a valuable pearl had been removed from the god's girdle ; and this proved to be the beginning of a series of remarkable thefts. Thenceforward, at intervals of twenty-eight days, as regularly as the moon waned, some gem or other would be found missing. Large rewards for information were freely offered by the temple authorities, the bolts were strengthened, the locks were changed, the guard was doubled, but still the thefts went on ; and although special measures were adopted by the police, the best efforts of the force had hitherto been unavailing.

On my arrival at Sungamkondah I called upon the Durmakurta, or temple guardian. He was a portly old Brahmin, with a fine sense of his own importance, and a very imperfect perception of mine; but I cared very little for that, the object of my visit being to secure the removal of the big diamond to a safer place than the temple. But he was obdurate.

"It would be sacrilege," he cried indignantly, "to extract the diamond from the sacred brow. Move the god bodily! Why, if it were even seriously spoken of, he would smite the town with small-pox. Besides, where is there a safer place than the temple?" and he added, with an air of scornful incredulity: "Who will dare to touch the sacred diamond?"

"Well, for the matter of that," I interposed, "who was it that dared to touch the sacred pearl, and the sacred emerald, and the lapis lazuli, and the turquoise, and the cat's-eye?"

He waved his hand haughtily as he replied, "They say all that was the work of a Rishi."

"And who or what is a Rishi?" I asked.

"A Rishi is a very holy being, more than a thousand years old, who dwells in the most inaccessible regions of the rocks, and is seldom seen by man."

"Has anybody seen *this* Rishi?" I inquired, with a smile.

"Yes," answered the old man sternly, "this Rishi has been seen. Penthiah, the poojary, has seen him, and has addressed him, speaking to him in Sanskrit; but the only reply vouchsafed was a glance that caused Penthiah to lie prostrate with ague for a fortnight. Yet even the Rishi will not venture to touch the sacred diamond."

Failing to obtain the aid I had hoped for, I proceeded to the temple, and caused all the priests and attendants to be assembled.

A long and careful examination of these worthies satisfied me that no conceivable precaution had been omitted, beyond, perhaps, that of making some one sleep near the image inside the building; but although the fame of the god extended over many districts, his abiding place was an evil-smelling, ill-ventilated structure about ten feet by twelve; and to require a man to pass a night in such a dungeon with closed doors would have been to insure his suffocation.

The bars and locks were new and powerful, and the keys, four in number, were at night lodged each with a separate custodian, the great key of the outer gate being deposited with the Durmakurta. The temple, as well as the high walls that surrounded it, was built of massive stone; and several watchmen patrolled the inner court, both by day and night. Unless the entire lot, Durmakurta, key-keepers, priests, poojaries, and watchmen were in the swim, it was impossible for a stranger to pass the threshold.

Dismissing the rest of the temple establishment, I desired Penthiah to remain, and when we were alone I questioned him closely concerning the strange being referred to by Durmakurta.

He described the Rishi as an ancient man of terrifying aspect, with a wrinkled skin hanging loosely upon a gaunt frame-work, and with matted hair and beard trailing on the ground, long curved nails, like the claws of a bird of prey, and deep sunken eyes, which not only glowed like live coals, but emitted a baleful heat that caused the object of their regard to feel as though muscle, nerve. and brain were dissolving into vapour.

Twice when the poojary was on guard at the temple door had this horrible creature appeared to him, and on the morning succeeding each visitation another valuable jewel was missed from the idol.

The last theft had taken place exactly twenty-seven days before the present interview, and, according to what might now be regarded as an established precedent, the monthly outrage upon the Swami was to be expected that very night.

Having ascertained these particulars, I determined to mount guard myself, and entering the temple court at sundown, I took up my post in front of the threatened shrine.

It is dreary work pacing up and down at night with nothing audible but one's own footsteps, and nothing visible but the stars. After a very few hours of it, eyes grow heavy, and limbs become weary; so about three o'clock I sat down to rest a little, leaning my back against the temple door. I did not know that sleep was stealing over me, or I would have got up and shaken it off by a brisk walk; but so it was, and when I opened my eyes the East was reddening with the dawn.

I arose, and carefully examined the bolts and bars; everything was in its place, and the seals upon the locks were intact. I accordingly rejoiced that I had no cause to reproach myself for my chance surrender to a common weakness.

When the priests came to open the door in order to make the ordinary morning offerings of flowers, I told them confidently that they would find their treasures safe, at any rate this time. But I was grievously deceived; a very valuable sapphire that had formed a pendant to Akasaramana's right ear had disappeared. I was fairly nonplussed; but worse was to follow.

Another month passed, and I again went to my post, this time after fortifying myself against drowsiness by an afternoon sleep and a heavy draught of black coffee.

I had just heard the stroke of two from a neighbouring gong when a light sound from inside the temple fell upon my ear. I inclined my face against the door, and, sure enough, I could discern a delicate click as though some sharp instrument were being cautiously driven into hard concrete. The thief was at work, but he was trapped. Hastily arousing the watchmen, who, after their manner were sleeping heavily, I made them surround the building, into which it seemed to me that the thief must have entered by the roof; I then despatched some one to bring the custodians of the keys; it was, however, several hours before I could secure the presence of these magnates, but in the meantime I never stirred from my position at the door.

When all the custodians had assembled, the sun was rising, and the priests were approaching with their flowers. "Here is your thief," I exclaimed triumphantly to the old Durmakurta, as I produced a pair of handcuffs from my pocket. The door swung open, and I pointed into the interior. "Bring him out," I ordered.

The Durmakurta adjusted his spectacles. "Where is the thief?" he inquired blandly; "I cannot perceive him."

The place was empty!

Four weeks later I was returning from a tour through my division. The country being new to me I had lost my way, and it was not till long past midnight that I found myself in the neighbourhood of Sungamkondah.

When I had come within a hundred yards or so of the Akasaramana temple, I nearly ran up against a heap of ruins that lay in my path. It was so dark that I had to pull up my horse and strike a fusee in order to see what lay in front of me. The brief blaze lighted up the surroundings for the space of several yards, and just as the flame died out, I saw—standing not ten paces from me—the Rishi! just as Penthiah had described him,—hide, hair, beard, claws, and all, but I did not observe the flaming eyes. I spurred my horse forward, and in another moment we were rolling over a block of masonry. I rose to my feet half-stunned, and it was some moments before I could recover myself sufficiently to remount; by that time, however, there were no indications to guide pursuit.

The next day the usual periodic theft was reported. This time the missing stone was an exquisitely coloured amethyst that I had observed only the week before flashing on the idol's shoulder.

It was to be remarked that as yet the Rishi had not abstracted two stones of the same sort; he evidently delighted in variety, and the sole constant feature of his depredations was the regularity of their recurrence. The only stones remaining now untouched were the large ruby and the sacred diamond.

Twenty-eight days after the foregoing incident, without declaring my intentions to any one, I took up my ground near the ruins. I had with me a good dark-lantern, which I flashed every minute or so in all directions. Judging by the stars, it might have been half-past one, when, on flashing my light for the hundredth time, I saw stealing away in the direction of the mountain the shadowy form of the Rishi.

I followed with great caution, keeping just within ear-shot of his footsteps, which, as the ground was covered with loose stones, was not difficult to accomplish. Suddenly the sound of his progression ceased ; and I found that I had arrived at the hill, which on this side was formed of a great shelving sheet of rock, some hundreds of yards high, and impracticable to any but naked feet.

Hastily divesting myself of my boots, I slowly ascended to a considerable height in the dark, and then, turning on my lantern, I swept the hill from base to summit. Far away near the crest stood the Rishi, but as I gazed he vanished behind a projecting ledge. Further pursuit was useless, but I felt that I was one step nearer the solution of the mystery.

Next day I received a report of the loss of the ruby, and the notification was accompanied by a harsh letter from the Durmakurta, saying that he was about to recommend my superintendent to remove me for gross and continued neglect of duty. The threat did not trouble me much ; I had a bit of a clue now, and there were four weeks in which to work it out. But things were drawing to a culmination ; unless the Rishi abandoned his practice of not taking two stones of the same sort, there was nothing now left to steal but the big diamond, which the thief had worked up to by a regular climax of depredation, and if the diamond went, I knew that I should probably be removed in disgrace.

During the twenty-eight days that were left to me I spent most of my time in roaming about the mountain, for I was convinced that the key to the mystery was to be found there, and there alone. My other duties I simply allowed to slide. One day, as I was climbing over a sort of hillock, the ground beneath me suddenly gave way, and I fell into a large cave. In one corner was a faint gleam of light, which proved to come from the entrance; and as I emerged into the sunshine, I found myself standing on the edge of the sheet of rock up which I had seen the Rishi climbing. Had it not been for this lucky accident I might have searched that great rocky bush-clad mountain for a year before I chanced upon the discovery.

Within the space of half an hour I had explored every nook and cranny of the cave; to all appearance it was empty, and I was about to depart, when my eye fell upon a *long white hair* that seemed growing out of the rock; closer inspection proved that the hair was kept in its place by a broad stone; this I easily removed, and found that it served to close a small aperture in which were concealed a large false beard, behind which were rolled up an enormous horse-hair wig, an old tattered gaberdine, and a pair of long leather gauntlets furnished with formidable claws. The mystery was now in a fair way of solution. My plan was soon formed, but I kept it to myself.

On the evening of the twenty-eighth day, having furnished myself with some phosphorus, I made my way cautiously to the cave. On arriving there I donned the Rishi's dress and appurtenances, and having rubbed the phosphorus liberally upon the walls of the cavern, I lighted my pipe, and sat down to await events.

At about eleven o'clock I heard the sound of heavy breathing outside—evidently that pull up the face of the rock was a trying one. Then came the crunch of a step upon the gravel at the entrance to the cave, and in another moment appeared the dark and indistinct figure of a man.

On seeing him I rose to my feet, and extending my arms began slowly to approach him. I anticipated a sharp struggle, and was prepared for it; but the background of lambent flame and the unexpected appearance of what seemed to him to be the real Simon Pure, was too much for the stranger's nerves. He uttered a loud cry, and fell forward senseless.

I rolled him upon his back, and, turning my

lantern on his face, beheld to my intense astonishment the features of the Durmakurta !

After a moment's consideration I determined upon adopting with him a course different from that which I should have followed in the case of an ordinary offender. Maintaining the *rôle* of the Rishi, I took a lump of phosphorus, and, kneeling down, traced in large characters upon his chest the word *Donga,* which in Telugu signifies "thief," then, leaving him to recover at his leisure, I proceeded to carry into execution the remainder of my project. Making my way to the temple, I got over the wall by the aid of two bamboos, with which I was provided, and walked warily towards the shrine.

At the door-way, snoring heavily, lay Penthiah, the poojary. Placing my hand upon his forehead I bade him arise ; he opened his eyes, but, as I had anticipated, seemed in no degree disconcerted at seeing a Rishi bending over him.

" Why have you not come by the secret passage ? " he asked, yawning.

"Because it is blocked, my son," I whispered in Telugu. " Come, help me to clear the way."

He arose sluggishly, and shouldering a ladder that lay hidden in the long grass behind the shrine, unsuspectingly led me over the wall to the heap of ruins.

After searching about for a few moments he stooped, and lifted a large flat stone.

"There is no obstruction," he muttered, as he peered into the cavity below; "the way is clear, my father, you can descend."

"Good," I replied, in a low voice, "return to the temple!" an order which, half asleep though he was, he was not slow to obey.

Descending into the hole I turned on my lantern, and saw that I was in a stone vaulted passage of great antiquity and much out of repair. Proceeding for about a hundred yards, I came to some steps at the top of which was another flat stone, which, working on a hinge, yielded to a push, and I found myself in front of the shrine. I directed my bull's-eye to the idol, and a brilliant gleam told me that the diamond was undisturbed. I had seen enough, and being satisfied that the gem was safe against any attempt that night, I returned to my quarters.

The next day I sought an interview with the Durmakurta, but was told that he was down with fever, and was too ill to be disturbed. As I turned to go I ran against the poojary. "Whither so fast, my friend?" I asked.

"The Durmakurta desires my presence on emergent business in connection with the temple," he answered, as he tried to pass me.

"The Durmakurta is too ill to see anybody," said I. "Come to my house. I, too, have to discuss with you emergent business connected with the temple" and I took his arm.

Finding resistance unavailing, the poojary doggedly accompanied me. Leading him into my private room, I closed the door.

"Was there a theft from the temple last night?" I asked.

"No," was the somewhat relieved reply.

"Did you not see the Rishi?"

"No," said the poojary, regarding me suspiciously.

"Then how did that saintly person remove the stone of the secret passage?"

He turned green with terror, and I thought I saw my chance.

"Where are the precious stones that have been removed from the idol during the past year and a quarter?"

But he instantly recovered himself, and, assuming

an air of stolidity, replied : "The stones ? Ah ! I wish I could tell you. Who knows the secrets of Rishis ?"

"*I* know them, and I arrest you as an abettor of systematic burglary," I answered, as I clapped a pair of handcuffs on his wrists.

Before the week was over I had prevailed upon the managers of the temple to call together all the people who were in any way connected with its administration. The number was too great to admit of their being all brought together in my house, so the meeting was held in the temple compound

Among those present, though much against his will, was the Durmakurta. He looked wasted and haggard, and was, in fact, so ill that he had to be provided with a chair.

In the back-ground was Penthiah, ironed, and escorted by two constables.

All being assembled, and the doors of the court-yard closed, I addressed the meeting in my choicest Telugu. I said that during the space of many months a great sacrilege had been going on, a sacrilege so artfully conducted that the discovery of its perpetrators had baffled the intelligence of man ; but what ingenuity could enable sin to foil the vengeance of the gods! At last Akasaramana had arisen in his wrath, and had commanded a sacred Rishi from the hills to avenge his outraged shrine. The thief, I continued, had been permitted for a time to pursue his impious course unscathed, but when his hand was raised to violate the sacred diamond he was branded on the breast by a finger of fire. The thief is in this assembly; it is not for me to point him out, let the writing of the god reveal him. Lay bare, all of you, your breasts, and prove your innocence to the world.

Thus adjured, every one, except the Durmakurta, at once threw aside his upper cloth.

"Respected father," I said gently, "be pleased to show us that you also are guiltless of this deadly sin."

But the old man had sunk backwards in his chair, and was gazing into the sky with the vacant stare of death.

Ever since that awful night upon the mountain he had believed that the hand of an offended god had fallen upon him, and that his days were numbered; from that hour his decline had been rapid, and the present ordeal had proved more than his enfeebled frame could bear.

One of the by-standers uncovered the old man's

chest in a vain endeavour to revive him, and there, seared into the flesh, were the fatal characters.

Calling the poojary to the front, I pointed to the dead man. " See," I cried, " how Heaven rewards the violators of its shrines; *that* traitor made no sign, and is now in *Nerekum ;* * as for *you* I can see already growing upon your forehead a fiery scroll in which *your* sins also are set forth. Confess ere it be too late where you have hidden the stolen jewels."

" The well," he gasped—" the dry well in the corner of the court."

Search was immediately made, and in an old tin box concealed among the rubbish at the bottom of the well lay the plundered regalia.

The Durmakurta assumed that particular disguise as a protection against possible capture, for the boldest man would hesitate to tackle a Rishi; the other circumstances were of course designed to further the idea of supernatural agency. A professional thief would have come at uncertain periods, and would probably have taken the pick of the basket at his first visit.

Poojary Penthiah got seven years.

* Hell.

A BLACK PRINCE.

THE Resident of Lilipatam had completed his monthly
inspection of the civil dispensary, and, accompanied
by the honorary surgeon in charge, was moving with
measured steps and dignified deportment towards the
outer door.

"What are you going to do with that long-legged
son of yours, Mr. Manuel?" inquired the Resident,
pausing on the threshold and regarding the honorary
surgeon with stately condescension.

The honorary surgeon smiled weakly and played
with a stethoscope that he was carrying.

"When a lad has turned twenty, it is high time
he was out in the world," continued the Resident.
"Why, I was earning my own living at eighteen."

At the very idea of the Resident of Lilipatam
finding himself under the necessity of working for
his living, Mr. Manuel's smile expanded into a
deprecatory grin. And as he grinned he displayed a

set of excellent teeth that gleamed the whiter by contrast with the dark olive of his ample cheeks.

"What are you going to do with him?" repeated the Resident.

"I thought of making him either a doctor, sir, or a liyar," replied the surgeon.

"A what?"

"A liyar, sir—a pleader."

"Oh, you mean a lawyer. You should be more accurate in your pronunciation. No, he is too big a fool for a lawyer; let him stick to his father's trade. Send him to England and make him walk the hospitals. Good day to you." As he spoke, Mr. Magnus mounted his dog-cart, and acknowledging the doctor's low bow by a curt nod, drove back to the Residency.

Mr. Magnus did not often deign to interest himself in the affairs of his subordinates, and the few chance words spoken that morning sank deeply into the mind of the honorary surgeon. Acted upon promptly and intelligently, the advice thus given might eventually constitute a claim upon the Resident's good offices. The value of a powerful patron was known to few men more clearly than to Mr. Manuel;—had not he himself, a poor Eurasian orphan, been taken by the hand when a child by a

large-hearted planter, who had given him as good an
education as the circumstances of the time permitted,
and had ultimately obtained for him an appointment
to the Indian Medical Service ? True, the nomina-
tion was to the lowest of the subordinate
grades, and it was by his own steady perseverance
and plodding industry that the planter's *protégé* had
attained his present position, but it was to his
patron that he owed the start. Why should the son
not begin where the father ended—nay, why should
he not begin a step higher and enter the commissioned
ranks ? Delirious thought, but withal possible.
Joseph was shy and timid, somewhat inclined to self-
indulgence and averse from work ; but Mr. Magnus
was wrong in his estimate of the lad's mental calibre,
he was certainly not a fool.

Exactly a month after the conversation at the
dispensary, a tall, shambling, whitey-brown youth
entered the Resident's private room. Although Joseph
came by appointment, Mr. Magnus was not present
to receive him. The gorgeously dressed peon who
discharged the office of door-keeper stated that the
Resident Sahib had not returned from his morning
drive, and that Mr. Joseph Manuel was to await him
in the private room.

The visitor's appearance was not prepossessing; his loose and lanky frame was clad in thin jail-made cloth of a grey-green hue; his scraggy neck was girt with a soiled collar encircled by a pale blue tie, and his splay feet were encased in clod-hopping boots. In one hand he held his hat—a large oval structure of pith and canvas—and in the other he grasped a thick bamboo walking-stick. His long black hair was radiant with oil, his brown face streamed with perspiration, and his languid eyes were heavy as though from recent tears.

Selecting a chair that, judged by its rigid and uninviting appearance seemed set apart for the accommodation of persons of the baser sort, he seated himself diffidently on its verge, and drawing forth a small pocket-handkerchief, proceeded to mop and scour his face.

The roll of approaching wheels was now heard, and a moment or two later a carriage drew up under the porch, then there was a rattling of bits and curb-chains, a patting of horses' necks, and a pawing of hoofs eager for the stable. As the carriage was led away, the voice of Mr. Magnus broke upon the ear; he was speaking with asperity, he was annoyed. Mr. Magnus suave and mannerly was sufficiently trying to weak nerves, but that gentleman moved to anger was dread and direful to the strongest. Joseph rose trembling, and stood, hat and stick in hand, gazing at the door.

Mr. Magnus entered hurriedly, with some official papers in his hand; he glanced sharply at Joseph and told him to be seated, then standing at the writing-table he took up a large blue pencil and began to endorse remarks upon the documents. Seeing that Joseph remained standing, he testily repeated his command that his visitor should take a chair.

In complying with the mandate, Joseph let his stick fall with a thud upon the floor, and in his effort to recover it nearly parted company with his hat. Mr. Magnus frowned at this display of clumsiness, and the delinquent experienced a sensation of faint-ness coupled with a desire for fresh air and solitude.

Mr. Magnus, having finished writing, solemnly enthroned himself in his great chair, crossed his legs, and tapped his knee gracefully with his gold-framed glasses.

Joseph Manuel perched on the extreme edge of his uncomfortable seat, and tightly grasping his hat and stick, regarded the great man with cataleptic terror. He had never before held converse with the Resident, indeed, his intercourse with that gentleman had been confined to obeisances in the public thoroughfares, or humble replies to patronizing inquiries at the dispensary; and here he was in the royal sanctum, enjoying the privilege of a private interview, and seated, actually seated, in the presence of the king!

His reflections were disturbed by a rasping voice from the chair of state. Mr. Magnus was haranguing him, and the tone of the speaker resembled that of a judge addressing a criminal whom he had determined upon hanging.

"Joseph Manuel, you are about to take the most important step in a young man's life. You are about to embark in a career, useful, honourable, and—ahem! lucrative. I am gratified to learn that my counsel has had due weight with your father; let it have equal influence with yourself. My advice to you is to keep out of debt, work hard, beat all your competitors, and remember the words of the Roman poet—

"'Qui studet optatam cursu contingere metam
Multa tulit fecitque puer, sudavit et alsit.'

"Sudavit et alsit," repeated Mr. Magnus, as Joseph Manuel mopped himself.

"You are going to England," continued the

speaker, "far away from the acquaintances of your youth"—

Joseph blew his nose.

"Far away from your relatives"—

Joseph sniffled.

"Far away from home and all its sunny memories"—

Joseph sobbed.

"Don't be a child," interrupted the Resident harshly. "What are you crying for?—a great hulking fellow like you crying!"

"I'm going to a place where I've no friends, no ac—ac—acquaintances, no ho—o—o—me," moaned Joseph.

Mr. Magnus waved his hand majestically.

"Dismiss all such craven repinings. I shall entrust you with a letter to Mrs. Magnus, to whom you are at liberty to pay your respects at her house in Kensington. I will write the letter now." And wheeling his chair to the table, he wrote as follows:—

"Dear Marian,

"The bearer is Joseph Manuel, the son of the honorary surgeon in charge of our dispensary—a very worthy old Eurasian whom I have known for many years. The lad is beginning his studies for the Medical Department ; he is a boor, an idler, and a fool. In England he will be as helpless as a sick monkey. Show him a little attention, and, if you and the girls can stand him, have him up now and then to Sunday tea.

" Your affectionate husband,

" LEMUEL MAGNUS."

Sealing the envelope with the Magnus peacock, he rose and handed the missive to the young Indo-Briton, who received it with due servility.

" Here is the letter," said Mr. Magnus, " and now farewell to you," and he extended two fingers.

Joseph clasped the proffered digits with fervid deference, and placing the precious document in his pocket, slunk home along the dusty pathway under the shade of the Persian trees like a man in a dream.

On turning the corner at the end of the broad avenue leading from the Residency, Joseph's ear caught the rattle of rapidly approaching wheels and hoofs. Recognizing in the sound the advent of a familiar but nevertheless keenly-favoured pageant, he ascended a heap of stones by the wayside in order the better to behold the spectacle. In a few moments some half-dozen horsemen clothed in gay but grimy habiliments and mounted on ill-fed and worse-groomed country-bred horses, cantered past him in picturesque disorder. They were followed at a short distance by a four-horse coach, painted yellow, with a huge coat of arms sprawling across the panels. On the box was a long-bearded Mohammedan coachman who worked his team more with his voice than with whip and reins. Inside the vehicle was a stolid-looking youth in a blue silk jacket and a gold-embroided cap. He was of about the same age and colour as Joseph, but somewhat fatter in face and more Paphian in eye. This was the Rajah of Lilipatam, at whose court Mr. Magnus represented the might and majesty of the suzerain power.

The monarch, who was engaged in chewing areca-nut, vouchsafed to young Manuel's salute the acknowledgment of a dull stare and a slow movement of the hand. He passed on, and the carriage was succeeded by more ill-clad and unwashed horsemen seated on fluffy steeds.

As the *cortège* with its enveloping dust-cloud disappeared round the corner, Joseph, stung with admiring envy, smote his stony pedestal with his stick and mused aloud :—

"Oh, to be a Rajah! and to have lacs and lacs of rupees, with all sorts of curries, the best of sweets, and fruit and liqueurs, and nothing to do but eat and drink, smoke and sleep, ride in a coach"—he called it a cooch—"and marry the prettiest women in the place. And best of all, always to stay at home—while I—I have to go away thousands, millions of miles to earn my daily rice."

Oppressed by the bitterness of his reflections, he belaboured the heap of stones with much severity, and then, descending to the foot-way, resumed his slouch in the direction of his father's house.

Turning into a weedy and arid enclosure laid out as a garden and surrounded by a wall of sun-dried mud, he entered a rambling white-washed house with a thatched roof and green, sun-blistered Venetian blinds. A hum of voices and the click of cutlery from an inner room informed Joseph that the family were at breakfast. Briskly hanging his hat on a peg in the verandah, the young man opened the door and joined the social gathering.

Joseph's family circle consisted of the honorary surgeon, that gentleman's wife, a pursy old lady of bistre hue, and five terra-cotta children whose respective ages ranged from seven to thirteen; those that had filled the gap between the eldest of these and Joseph had been nipped in their early bloom.

When Joseph entered the room the honorary surgeon was distributing curry to the family from a capacious bowl. He paused in the exercise of this patriarchal function, and regarding his son and heir with grave anxiety, inquired how he had sped.

" First-rate," replied Joseph, with a heavy wink.

" Well done, my boy. What did he say to you ? "

" Give me some curry and rice, and then I'll tell you," replied Joseph, holding out a plate for his share of the savoury compound. His father piled his plate and his mother filled his cup. An expectant silence, broken only by the prattling of the little ones, was maintained by the party while the heir of the house broke his fast. At length Joseph, who although a worm in the presence of Mr. Magnus was a vertebrate animal in his own family, condescended to satisfy the general curiosity.

" He has given me a letter to Mrs. Magnus."

" To Mrs. Magnus ! " exclaimed his mother delightedly.

" Ah, to Mrs. Magnus, and told me to call on her at Ken—Kensinpatam, and she's got to be kind to me."

K

" Why, I rec'lect her, 'Dolphus," said Mrs. Manuel, addressing her husband, " I rec'lect her when she stayed at the Residency last Christmas five years, and she was the haughtiest haughtiest I ever see. You remember her, surely ? "

But Mr. Manuel did not reply, his thoughts were with his son.

" My dear boy, you'll do well—a good beginning, that letter. I s'pose she'll introduce you to the Surgeon-General, and the Lord Mayor, and the Bishop of St. Paul's, and "—Mr. Manuel's knowledge of London failed to carry him further, so he concluded comprehensively, "the rest of the Government officers."

" Josey will be coming back quite a Europe gentleman," observed the child of thirteen.

" So he will, Chustie, and with a moustache and gold lace down his trousers," smiled the honorary surgeon, whose fine teeth had never ceased to beam upon his first-born since the mention of the letter.

" And with a blue-eyed wife, I'll be bound," added his mother, with a waggish leer.

"Let us see the letter, Josey, boy," said his father. And the Resident's missive was delved for, and exhumed from Joseph's breast-pocket.

Having been made to perform sundry flourishes in the air expressive of high triumph, it was handed round for admiring inspection. The hand-writing, the paper, the seal, and the general appearance were minutely criticized; the seniors weighed the envelope and the juniors solemnly smelt it. Finally, the honorary surgeon held it up to the light in the hope that some of the verbal treasures within might be visible through the covering. Clearly, the Resident's caution in affixing the peacock seal was not misplaced; gum could be managed, but, as Mrs. Manuel observed, sealing-wax was troublesome.

When the billet was returned to its possessor, the general verdict was that it looked very business-like and was worth to Joseph at least a thousand rupees.

A few days later the young adventurer was lying horribly sea-sick in a second-class cabin on board the screw-steamer *Diver*, homeward bound from Bombay.

The voyage was uneventful. Joseph travelled from port to port with the listless unintelligence of a bullock ; the only mental exercise that he allowed himself was the devising of cunning plans for returning to India before the end of the year ; the rest of his time was spent in sea-sickness and tears.

At Southampton he presented a piteous spectacle

K 2

of helplessness, and it was solely owing to the good-nature of his cabin companion—a retired sergeant of dragoons—that he was able to gather his luggage together and take train for London.

Joseph Manuel's luggage consisted of three wooden cases : the first contained wearing apparel ; the second, curry-powder for his sustenance while in England ; and the third, several dozen bottles of omum-water, distilled by his father and regarded by that veteran practitioner as a sovereign prophylactic against the harmful vapours of London town.

His first care on arriving in London was to find a lodging suited to his modest requirements, and after a day's desultory research he installed himself, together with his curry-powder and his omum-water, in two small rooms over a dingy shop in a back street near the British Museum. Then having paid his fees and complied with the necessary formalities, he commenced work as a student at St. Æsculap's Hospital.

Leaving him thus usefully employed we must for a short time return to Lilipatam, where Mr. Magnus, seated at early tea in the upper verandah, is enjoying the weekly treat of the Englishman in India—a ramp through the English mail. Letters, circulars, newspapers, and magazines are strewn in lavish profusion upon the wide table before him, and while, paper-knife in hand, he deliberates as to the first point of his attack, his eye falls upon the handwriting of Mrs. Magnus, and the sight of the familiar characters decides him.

Brevity has been declared to be the soul of wit, but some people hold profuseness to be the spirit of scripture; and if the apothegm is sound, Mrs. Magnus was an excellent correspondent. We have not space at command sufficient to reproduce the whole of her letter, but will extract a portion from the concluding page:

"After this account of our doings at York, you will not be surprised to hear that we are glad to get back to quiet Snooseby—especially Trelise. Jack Aventayle has been over to see us twice; the death of his Guardsman cousin leaves him now *third* for the peerage. Angelica has grown quite extravagant since she came into her three-hundred a year, and spends quite a fortune on dress. Her last exploit was to buy a forty-guinea frock at Descou's—light blue and pale pink. She certainly looks well in it, with her fair hair and clear complexion. . . . . As we are not in town this season, your East Indian

protégé posted your letter of introduction to me.
I shall show him what attention I can when
we go up in the winter, and have written to say we
shall be at the usual address in Kensington. . . . .
Mind and come home if you have any more trouble
with that horrid gout."

II.

A YEAR later Mrs. Magnus concluded her weekly
letter as follows : " Our party on Wednesday went
off very well. Lady Helmethame promised, but did
not come; we had, however, the Dudley-Jenkinsons
and the Trawlers, and other good people; about eighty
came out of a hundred-and-twenty asked. Jack
Aventayle spent the whole evening with Trelise—he
is now only *two* from the title. Young Mr. Manuel
played on the concertina, and sang—not at all well;
but as he was from India the people were interested.
They thought 'The Cottage by the Sea' was an
Indian ballad sung in the vernacular. A lady wrote
to me the next day asking as a great favour if I could

get her a copy of *Tha Khutaj bai thasi* from the Indian gentleman. Some people would have it that he was a Rajah—I believe that silly boy Aventayle was at the bottom of it. Mr. Manuel is a very quiet, well-behaved young man ; always ready to be of use to us. The girls rather sit upon him, but he takes it very good-naturedly."

Twelve months had elapsed since Joseph Manuel, limp, despairing, and unclean, had staggered from the lively deck of the good ship *Diver* to the more welcome footing of the Southampton quay.

The year in London had wrought a striking change both in the outer and the inner man of the exile. A drooping moustache now concealed his large flaccid lips ; his hair, no longer glistening with odorous unguents, was decently cut ; his clothes were well made, and set off his burly figure to advantage ; for Joseph the lanky, loose-set hobbledehoy had become actually burly. By a fortunate chance that befell shortly after his arrival in London, he discovered in a secluded corner of Bloomsbury a culinary temple in which the chief priest was a skilled composer of the spiced stew which in England counterfeits a curry. This accomplished artist understood, moreover, the preparation of kicheri and pilau, and of many other pungent and greasy aliments favoured in the East. Here thrice a day had Joseph feasted unctuously. His own private store of curry-powder he had sold at a handsome figure to the keeper of the restaurant, but had failed to induce that un-enterprising tradesman to extend his speculation to the omum-water.

After battening for a year upon stimulating and succulent confections, Joseph had begun to grow corpulent, and now presented to the careless eye the outlines of a stalwart man. Indeed, the Miss Mag-nuses were not indisposed, *faute de mieux*, to retain the services of so tall and portly a cavalier as escort in ordinary. It is true that there were points in him that still required improving: he was, perhaps, a little too fond of bright-coloured raiment; his taste for jewellery might with benefit have been chastened; and it was generally considered that his fondness for pat-chouli was misplaced. As has already been shown, Joseph had made the acquaintance of Mrs. Magnus, and had been advanced from five-o'clock teas to mid-night crushes. Society in England was at that time directing a drowsy attention to India, it was the year of the Prince of Wales' visit to our great dependency, and in certain quarters no evening party was considered complete without the presence of some ethnological specimen of the East, so Joseph found himself in request not only at the "at homes" of Mrs. Magnus, but at more ambitious entertainments at the houses of her friends. These extended experiences taught him to converse easily on the ordinary topics of the day, and invested him with a manner and a style that were greatly to his advantage.

It was a fine afternoon in July. Mrs. Magnus having been disappointed by a man who was to have made a fourth in her carriage, had bidden Joseph at the shortest notice accompany her and two of her daughters to Hurlingham.

Mrs. Magnus by means of rigid economy in her Yorkshire cottage during nine months of the year was able, when in London during the season, not only to give smart parties, but to allow herself a carriage. They were on the ground early, and fell into a good position near the pavilion, where they could observe the entrance of later arrivals and discuss the appearance of their friends.

"There's the Rawleys' drag, ma; it's got into the wrong place, and the policemen are turning it back," said Angelica Magnus, with animation. "Captain Rawley looks as though he would like to whip them."

"Here's Lady Helmethame, ma, dear," whispered Trelise, who sat by her mother's side, "and Mr. Aventayle's with her."

"Look at the Dudley-Jenkinsons," cried Angelica, "with their new team of bays. Oh, what lovely horses! Who are those two girls with the wonderful hats?"

"They are the Duke of Cranberry's daughters, Lady Betty and Lady Moggy Tartlet, great friends of Flora Dudley-Jenkinson," replied Mrs. Magnus, who knew most people about town—by sight.

"Mr. Aventayle's coming this way, ma, dear. May I walk with him if he asks me?" whispered Trelise.

"Yes, dear, but only for an half an hour; and remember not to eat strawberries in that frock—recollect what happened to your mauve at the Orleans."

"Do you know what this match is?" inquired Joseph, who felt rather out of the conversation and wanted to say something.

"Oh, the Blues and the Lancers, or the Greys and the Inniskillings, I forget which," replied Mrs. Magnus absently. "How de do, Mr. Aventayle? What a time they are beginnin'; I suppose they're waitin' for the Princess, though." Mrs. Magnus always dropped her *g's* when she had her quality manner on.

" Here she is," said Aventayle, turning and lifting his hat as the Marlborough House carriage swept by. The ladies bent low, but Joseph, who had never before been in such close neighbourhood to British royality, was so dazzled by the kindly smile from the passing victoria that he forgot to bow to its gracious occupants, and recovered himself in time only to bestow a humble salutation upon an out-rider in the rear.

After exchanging greetings with the ladies, Aventayle turned to Joseph, with whom he already had a how-d'ye-do acquaintance, and asked him to go for a stroll. Joseph, whose long legs were becoming painfully cramped in the carriage, readily complied. As they walked away Aventayle remarked :—

" My aunt, Lady Helmethame, wants me to introduce you to her ; she wants to hear about India. Do you mind ? "

Joseph had no objection to offer, and the young men turned towards a barouche manned by a fat coachman with a short curly wig, and two footmen with heavily-powdered hair.

" I say," Aventayle went on, "my aunt believes you're a Rajah ; it's a capital joke—mind you keep it up." And before Joseph could reply he found himself standing at a carriage-door and bowing to two elderly ladies, one of whom was addressing him.

"I am delighted to know you, Rajah. The Duchess of Daylesford—" and she glanced towards the lady at her side—" also wishes to become acquainted with you. Duchess, this is the Rajah of— ? "

" Liliput ! " supplied Aventayle.

" No, you silly boy ; that's in Gulliver's Travels. What is it, Rajah, that they call your place—your dominions, I should say ? "

" Lilipatam," stammered Joseph, lifting his hat to the Duchess, and feeling very hot and choky.

" The Rajah of Lilipatam," continued Lady Helmethamc, "and he is now in England studying—— ? " and she looked inquiringly at Aventayle.

" The sanitary and therapeutic systems of the British Isles," responded her nephew.

" Insanity and the reputed systems of the British Isles," repeated the old lady. " And now, Jack, we will release you ; we want to have a long talk with His Highness—so, dear boy, *au revoir !* "

"I have had many friends in India," began the Duchess, in a weary voice; "some of my relatives have been Governors of Presidencies. Did you ever meet Lord Tresby—no?—ah! he was perhaps a little before your time, but you would have known my cousin Stranraer; he commanded the army of occupation in—ah! I always forget your terrible Indian names—it begins with a *B*, or a *D*, or a *C*, and ends with *pore* or *abad*. Did you know him? Such a nice fellow, so fond of sport; a fine rider, and, I have heard, a first-rate soldier. I am sure you would have liked him. Talking of sport, are you giving the Prince any tiger-shooting? or does he not go to Lillypore?"

"N—no—no. I have not heard that he is expected in our part of India," bleated Joseph.

"Oh no, Duchess," interposed Lady Helmethame. "If the Prince had been expected at Lillybad, we should not have the pleasure of seeing the Rajah in England—should we, Rajah?"

Joseph smiled a ghastly smile, and faintly replied, "Certainly not."

Now, to do him justice, it must be stated that Joseph Manuel was not a willing accessory to this imposture; had he been allowed time to think, his fears would have safeguarded him. He was keenly alive to the folly of the position—he had not yet realized the danger of it—and would have given all he was worth to be able to laugh gaily, and gracefully explain how that incorrigible *farceur*, Jack Aventayle, was enacting a merry jest, and that he, Joseph, had for the moment allowed himself to fall into the humour of the frolic, but that in sober truth he was no lion, but only Snug the joiner. This he would have done had he possessed the power, but alas ! when he essayed it, he felt as though his nerves of volition were sheathed in lead, and he could no more have explained matters now than he could have lifted the barouche. He was as a man launched in a toboggan —he had no option but to sit tight and go forward.

As it happened, he found but little difficulty in sustaining the *rôle* thus unexpectedly thrust upon him. The conversation that ensued was entirely upon India. Its missions, its schools, its infant-marriages, its zenanas, its poverty, its wealth, all by turns received passing attention. Both ladies preferred talking to listening, and their knowledge of Indian subjects was so confused and indistinct, that Manuel's immature pronouncements and hesitating confirmation

of their own nebulous theories passed as the utterance
of a man who was profoundly conversant with every
detail of the administration.

Joseph stood by Lady Helmethame's carriage for
more than an hour; although conscious that he was
failing in his duty to the Magnus party, he did not
well know how to withdraw, and waited in the
Eastern manner for some hint of dismissal; but still
the ladies prattled on. Suddenly her Ladyship
exclaimed, "Look, the Princess is going to present
the cup. Rajah, the Duchess wants to see it given;
will you be good enough to escort Her Grace to the
pavilion? I shall stay in the carriage."

One of the powdered footman opened the door and
the Duchess descended. Joseph was at first doubtful
whether he should walk in front of her after the
manner of a chobdar clearing the way for the Rajah
of Lilipatam, or whether he should follow her like a
peon in attendance on Mr. Magnus; but as the old
lady talked to him without cessation, he concluded
that, after all, the proper place of the escort to a
Duchess was by his charge's side.

When, half-an-hour later, he bid Lady Helmethame and the Duchess good-bye, the latter expressed
a hope that he was not engaged on the following

Wednesday fortnight, as she particularly wished him to dine with her that evening.

After a decent show of memory exercise, Joseph discovered that his numerous engagements would not prevent his dining with the Duchess on the night in question, and this being satisfactorily established, he rejoined the Magnuses.

The return journey to London was performed in almost funereal silence. Mrs. Magnus was huffed. She had not brought this young man to Hurlingham in order that he might serve as squire to other dames. She and Angelica, poor things, had sat alone in the carriage from start to finish. Trelise had walked about for ten minutes or so with Jack Aventayle, who had afterwards been seen paying marked attention to a pretty girl in dark blue, believed to be an American and consequently dangerous, on the box-seat of a neighbouring drag.

Mrs. Magnus' next letter to her husband contained the following: " Jack Aventayle has most unexpect-edly become *next* for the peerage ! the present Earl can't last out the year. And I am convinced that when Jack is Lord Morion he will propose to Trelise . . . . That young Manuel is getting quite spoilt, and I'm sure is neglecting his studies."

III.

The Duchess's dinner party was remarkable for the quality rather than for the number of the guests. Among them were a German Prince and an English Duke, two ex-Cabinet Ministers, a highly distinguished and many-wounded old Cavalry General, a Bishop, an Earl, two Viscounts, and a lyric poet. There was also a due proportion of ladies, among whom was a certain cousin of Jack Aventayle's—one Lady Louisa Bever, poet, enthusiast, and ex-beauty, who bore her burden of thirty-seven summers with the vivacity of seventeen. It was for this lady's especial behoof that Joseph Manuel had been bidden to the board.

The guests had all assembled in the drawing-room, and the extreme limit of grace was on the point of being reached, when the doors were thrown open and the head footman announced in sonorous accents " 'Is 'Ighness the Rajjer of Lilybedam."

There was a general turning of heads in the direction of the door, and the curiosity of the assembly was amply rewarded by the spectacle that met their gaze.

A tall and portly person of olive complexion and stately presence advanced slowly into the room and bowed; he was clothed in the flowing robes of an Eastern king; his enormous turban sparkled with diamonds, gems gleamed from his embroidered waist-belt, from his short dagger, from the hilt of his long curved sword, from his fingers, from his forehead, from his ears—from wherever it was possible to attach a jewel there shot a luminous ray.

Coruscating as he moved, he advanced another pace or two and bowed to the Duchess, who, holding out her hand, exclaimed, "Rajah, it is so good of you to oblige me;" and, lowering her voice a little, she added, "Mr. Aventayle tells me that you do not wish to be treated *en roi*, so I shall sacrifice my own vanity and go down to dinner with Prince Von Tapferkeit, magnanimously surrendering you, Rajah Manool, to my cousin, Lady Louisa Bever."

The introduction was barely accomplished when dinner was announced, and the company descended to the dining-room.

It may be asked whether Joseph Manuel had suddenly qualified for admission to the Colney Hatch lunatic asylum, that he appeared in public

thus disguised: the circumstance certainly requires
explanation. The way it came about was this: On
her way back from Hurlingham, the Duchess expressed satisfaction that she had secured the Rajah
for her dinner-party, and added a hope that he might
be induced to attend in his royal robes, for dear
Louisa was coming, and Louie did so love "barbaric
pearl and gold." Whereupon Jack Aventayle, regarding the draping of Joseph as a step that would
render the jest more excellent than ever, had undertaken to convey the proposal to the "Rajah."

On the following afternoon by a happy chance
meeting Joseph turning from the Park into Piccadilly,
he took him into the Naval and Military Club for a
smoke and a quencher. Before they had got half
through their cigars Aventayle had persuaded his
companion to humour the Duchess. It was, he urged,
merely an innocent masquerade that need never be
repeated; and as for the costume, Abiram, the
theatrical property man in Wardour Street, would
supply it, together with any number of paste
diamonds and martial cutlery, for a sum of money
which he, Aventayle, would willingly provide;
indeed, he considered the expense to be a legitimate
charge upon him, seeing that it was owing to his

initiative that Manuel found himself in his present position.

Thus it was that the curiosity of the Duchess was gratified, and Lady Louisa Bever enjoyed the fulfilment of her darling aspiration—a *téte-à-téte* with an Eastern king.

"India simply fascinates me," began her Ladyship, as they descended the stairs. " Eastern travel has long been the dream of my life. Your voluptuous country, where the flowers ever blossom, the beams ever shine, with its wealth, its teeming population, its strange vegetation, its magnificent scenery, is to me as a fairy-tale, but a fairy-tale which is capable of being brought to the test of actual experience, and which I begin even now to realize. Now, do tell me, Rajah Manool, all about your gorgeous realm."

"Over how many millions do you wield the sceptre?" asked Lady Louisa, not waiting for a reply to her former remark. They had by this time sat down, and Joseph had begun his soup; he attentively examined his suspended spoon as though it were a calculating machine which the vastness of the computation made it necessary for him to consult; he then, in a dubious tone, uttered the monosyllable " um," and went on with his *consommé*.

Dearly as Joseph loved the carminative cookery of his native land, his palate was rapidly learning to appreciate very keenly the choicer productions of Western *chefs;* but he found his enjoyment of her Grace's good cheer sadly marred by the necessity of replying to the fusilade of questions maintained without intermission by the lady at his side.

" I suppose you rule many more than the entire population of Great Britain ? " continued his fair querist, looking full into her companion's brown face.

Compelled to reply, Joseph muttered something to the effect that possibly the number of his subjects was a few millions greater than that of the inhabitants of the British Isles.

" And the pomegranites, and the bulbuls, and the ' shrines of fretted gold, ' " proceeded Lady Louisa, in enthusiastic inconsequence; " and your unspeakable regalia ?   Oh, what splendid jewels you must have in your treasure-house ! " and she glanced admiringly on Abiram's paste.

Joseph grinned feebly as he fingered his pinchbeck rings.

" You smile: they are trifles to you, no doubt; but— thank you, champagne—but oh, what a treat to us

Europeans to gaze even for a few moments upon the rubies, emeralds, sapphires, diamonds, and pearls lying heaped in prismatic splendour on the floors of your palace vaults!"

Joseph stared at Lady Louisa, but, seeing that he was expected to say something, observed that he thought it must be "very prettee indeed."

"What I require," said Lady Louisa, "is information. I want facts, truths, certainties." Joseph winced. "I know so little of your marvellous country, and that little I have acquired by the most desultory reading——"

"Newspapers?" inquired Joseph.

"Oh, *no;* newspapers, essays, and books of travel I abjure. My teachers are the novelist and the poet. I once began to write a poem on India. I called it 'The Scimitar and the Sari.' It opens like this—

'"The moonlight rose from its couch on the sea,
It slid through the ivory arch,
And crept o'er the cedar floor;
While the breeze sighed low in the cypress tree,
And the Nubian guard held his weary march
In front of the golden door.'

"Do you employ Nubians for that purpose?" she asked, after Joseph had testified his admiration of what he called her "nice lines."

" For what purpose ? " inquired Manuel, who had failed to grasp the allusion.

" To—to guard the—palace, to keep watch and ward over you, and—and—yours at night. I suppose you always sleep in that romantic banana ? "

" I sleep in a banyan," replied Joseph, feeling now upon firmer ground.

" And your sultanas, I suppose there are many of them in Lilipatam ? "

" We don't call them sultanas out there," said Joseph ; and forgetting for the moment that he was posing as the Rajah added, " There are, of course, a good many women in the palace."

" O-oh ! " ejaculated Lady Louisa, much interested in the announcement. " Ah, poor things! I presume you keep them closely veiled and immured behind their gilded bars. Now, why, Rajah, did you not bring one or two of them with you to this country ? May I ask you the name of your favourite queen ? "

At that moment the Duchess rose, and Manuel was relieved from the embarrassment into which the last remark had thrown him.

When the ladies had withdrawn, a gentleman who had been sitting on the other side of Lady Louisa moved into her place. and, addressing Joseph,

observed, with a courteous smile, that he feared the
Rajah must find the climate of England very trying.

Joseph said that it was certainly colder than in
India.

"I have been somewhat intimately connected with
your country," continued the gentleman. "I was
once Under Secretary of State for India for a short
time, and have served on several Parliamentary Com-
mittees dealing with Indian affairs."

Joseph shuddered ; he felt cold all over.

"I spent a delightful fortnight last winter in Calcutta with the Viceroy. Do you know Lord Lytton?"

Joseph's shake of the head might have implied
that he was acquainted with his Lordship, but that
owing to strained relations between the Court of
Lilipatam and Fort William, his friendship with the
Governor-General was not so cordial as heretofore.

"I met some very interesting people in Calcutta,"
observed the politician ; "among them the Rajah of
Lacca, a highly educated and most intelligent man.
Do you know him? Ah, no—he lives in the North, and
you are from the South. There was also a most enter-
taining fellow—Babu something or other—the great
reformer—dear me, what is his name?" Joseph had
no suggestion to make, and the speaker went on.

" His fluency was remarkable, and his knowledge of English seemed to be perfect. They are wonderful orators, those Babus."

" Yes," said Joseph, " wonderful." Oh, if he could only talk like a Babu !

" Do you think now," asked the other, speaking very slowly and deliberately, "that it would be for the good of India if the people were granted representative government ? "

Joseph did not clearly understand the question, but at a venture replied " No," and tossed off a glass of wine.

" Precisely my own view," said the gentleman complacently; " but let me question you further. Why should they *not* have their representatives in Parliament—they are taxed ? "

Joseph turned upon his interlocutor a gaze of such plaintive misery that the latter. seeing he was causing his companion pain, remarked, with apologetic good humour, " I see, I see—you would rather not pursue this theme. Any expression of opinion from you would of course be of great weight and importance, and you would naturally prefer not to proclaim your views until the Imperial Government collects the sentiments of the great feudatories."

Joseph breathed more freely, and drank his fourth glass of the Duchess's '47.

"Now, tell me," said the statesman, speaking in a frank, confidential tone, "what do you think of your Resident, or your Political Agent, whatever you call him?"

"Do you mean Mr. Magnus?" asked Joseph, with some show of animation in his manner. "Do you mean Mr. Lemuel Magnus, C.I.E.?"

"Yes, Magnus is the name—Lemuel Magnus. I occasionally came across it in documents from the Viceroy when I was at the India Office. How do you get on with him—are you good friends?"

"No, we are not good friends," replied Joseph solemnly; the generous qualities of the royal wine were beginning to assert themselves, and he saw no reason why he should not deal a blow at the dreaded and hated autocrat five thousand miles away. "He treats me like the dirt under his feet—he is a stuck-up, swaggering, haughty beast!"

"Ah!" said the other softly, "I grieve to hear this, I grieve extremely to hear it; no Resident is worth his salt who cannot keep on good terms with his Prince. But I have no doubt that the fault rests with Magnus. From my experience of him when I was

Under Secretary, I could see that he was a difficult man to deal with ; far too arrogant and domineering —pardon me," they had risen to go upstairs, " if I ask you where a letter will find you—the Duchess tells me that you are at home almost *incog.*, you would, therefore, perhaps not wish any reference made to the India Office."

Joseph assured his friend that, on the whole, perhaps it would be better if the India Office were not troubled about his movements, and desired that communications should be sent him for the present to the care of the Honourable John Aventayle.

On entering the drawing-room Joseph found himself standing by the side of the German Prince in front of an arrangement of miniatures. Seeing this, the Duchess rose and joined them, saying with a pleasant glance at Manuel—

" I really must introduce you two royal personages to each other—Prince Von Tapferkeit and Rajah Manool will have much in common to talk about."

The two men bowed, and the Prince, speaking in a strong foreign accent, asked Joseph whether he had a large army.

" A very large one," replied Joseph, who had

drunk enough wine to make him reckless. "An enormous army."

"So!" ejaculated the German, regarding the other with much interest. "Then you are a man to be reckoned with."

Joseph opined that he certainly was not a negligable quality.

"Do you adopt the French or the English drill in your fine army?" asked the Prince.

"Oh, both — sometimes one, sometimes the other."

"Ah, change is goot, but it must not be too frequent. For the attack now, do you favour the column, the line, or the loose formation?"

"All, all," said Joseph, waving his hand comprehensively. "I like 'em all."

"*Ya wohl!* May I ask," continued the Prince, with a keen look of curiosity, "have you performed much campaign?"

"Do you mean have I drunk much champagne?"

"No; have you fought in wars and battles?"

"Nothing of that sort for me," said Joseph, shaking his head jocosely. "Why, if I found myself in a battle I should run away."

The Prince gazed at him steadily through his

pince-nez for a moment, and then resumed his examination of the miniatures.

Shortly afterwards the party broke up, and on returning to his rooms near the Museum, Joseph found the following letter awaiting him :—

"LILIPATAM, *June* 10*th*, 1878.

" MY DEAR JOSEPH,

" Your letters received since Christmas troubled me and your mother very much indeed. You are always complaining that reading and studying makes your head ache, and are always asking for more money that you may give yourself recreation. Do you think I am made of money ? I have told you again and again that the two hundred pounds a year which I allow you is part of a sum that I have been all my life saving for your education. If I increase your allowance I must cut short your time of study. What will happen then ? You will not pass for a doctor, and must serve in my dispensary as a dresser— and I hoping to see you a gentleman and married to an English lady. You complain of your debts. Why do you run them up ? Now, these are my last words to you. I am sending you a bill for £100 to pay your debts and put you straight, and this is the very last money that you will get from me besides your regular allowance, which, if you dare again to exceed it, shall be stopped and you re-called to Lilipatam.

" Mr. Magnus, your honoured patron, is leaving for England next week, and he has promised me to give you a good talking to. He will call for your accounts, so have them ready."

The letter concluded with domestic news, which, as it has no bearing upon our story, need not be repeated. Joseph, having carelessly read the missive through, laughed pot-valiantly and scrambled into bed.

When Manuel opened his eyes next morning the possible results of his fooling overnight at first dawned upon him but dimly. In the course of his reflections, however, certain complications that might conceivably ensue from his recent escapade presented themselves to his awakening mind more distinctly ; the leading thought, and it smote his brain as with a scourge, was that Mr. Magnus was coming to England, to London, to him. Slowly and painfully recalling the incidents of the preceding night, he told himself that he, humble Joseph Manuel, had, in a passing moment of unaccountable frenzy, vituperated the dread dictator in terms the very thought of which sent a thrill darting down his spinal marrow and vibrating through every nerve and ganglion in his body. He—the worm, the insect—had actually denounced the Resident at the Court of Lilipatam, and this to a stranger occupying a high social position and possessing enormous influence in the State by reason of his close and intimate connection with the Government. He recalled, too, with a clammy brow and a sinking heart, how this influential statesman had demanded and obtained his, the accuser's, address. Now, why did the powerful and illustrious unknown desire this information ? The reason was abundantly, luridly clear. What had been uttered by Joseph in his *rôle* of Indian sovereign would in the natural course of administrative routine be conveyed to Her Most Gracious Majesty the Indian Empress, with the inevitable result that Lemuel Magnus would be impeached for cruelty to his Rajah, and Joseph Manuel would be appointed chief prosecutor and leading witness.

Electrified by this preposterous figment of his imagination, Joseph bounded out of bed, and, clasping his large head with his hands, strode, in an agony of fear and remorse, up and down the room, moaning.

As he passed the table on which lay his father's letter, his eye fell upon the bill of exchange. Joy ineffable! There lay the means of escape. He would take ship and sail for India before the Resident arrived. He would place seas and continents between himself and Mr. Magnus. The intermission which this cheering thought gave to his lamentations enabled him to become aware of a knocking at his door which had been proceeding for several minutes.

"Who's there?"

"A gentleman wants to see you, sir."

Joseph's heart for a moment ceased to beat. Undoubtedly this was a messenger from the India Office, or from Parliament, or Windsor Castle.

"Out, out! I am out!" he shouted; "say I am on the Scotch hills, in the Irish jungles—for a week, a month."

"No, no, my boy. You're at home all right," said a voice that he recognized as Aventayle's. "May I come in?" and without more ado Jack opened the door and entered the room.

"I've come to hear how the show went off last

night; it must have been worth a ' thou.' to see— tell us all about it, old chappie."

Hastily disencumbering his only chair of the theatrical finery that had rendered him such questionable service, Joseph begged his visitor to be seated, then wrapping himself in an old dressing-gown, and squatting on his chest of omum-water, he proceeded to regale Aventayle with a prolix and lugubrious account of the dinner-party.

Aventayle laughed so uncontrollably at the recital, that the speaker was several times compelled to pause in order to allow his listener to recover himself sufficiently to hear what was said. That which especially delighted Jack was the account of Joseph's introduction as a brother royalty to the German Prince.

"I know Von Tapferkeit," he said; "never met such a keen soldier in all my life—and you pulled his leg—ha! ha! ha!—told him all about your army, and then said—ha! ha! ha!—that you always bolted out of action. Well, if that don't take the cake The sportsman you talked to at dessert must have been Warberry. Was he a tall, thin, cadaverous-looking Johnnie, with a bald head and a hooked nose ? "

" Yes."

" And wore an eye-glass ? "

" Yes."

"Oh, that was Warberry — Lord Warberry, Secretary of State for Feudatory Affairs; he'd be much interested in *you*, and I've no doubt is at this moment engaged in looking up Lilipatam in the gazetteer. What a score—what a score ! I bet you he sends for Magnus, and asks why you have not been taken to Court and regularly introduced into London society. He seemed to acquiesce in your *incognito*, did he ?—that's Warberry all over. He'll raise such a breeze about it at the India Office—enough to blow the clerks out of the windows. Hope he didn't ask for your address ? "

" Yes," replied Joseph hesitatingly " that's just what he did."

" You never gave it him ? "

" Oh, no. I told him to address to me care of you," replied Joseph, with a dubious smile.

" Whew ! " whistled the Honourable Jack ; and the perspiration gathered in beads on Joseph's brow.

There was a pause, and in the interval Jack lighted a cigarette ; he then suddenly observed—

" By the way, have you heard that old Magnus

turned up last night quite unexpectedly at Kensington? Doctors sent him off at short notice—gout I believe it was—and his letter to Mrs. Mag. miscarried. What are you going to do with yourself this next fortnight?"

Joseph had intended to spend part of the next fourteen days on the broad ocean, but with the foe at his very gates there was no time to make arrangements for the voyage; his sole consideration now was to secure his safety for the immediate hour, and when Aventayle proposed that our hero should accompany him to Clovenhelm—Lady Helmethame's place in Yorkshire—Joseph accepted the offer with almost abject gratitude.

"The only bother about it is this," continued Jack: "I must start at once, having to see that the house is ready for my aunt and a heap of visitors that she always has down at this time of year. In point of fact, my man has gone to the station with my kit, and I am now on my way to King's Cross. I suppose you will want a day or two longer in town to work off your engagements?"

Joseph hastened to assure his friend that on no account would he miss the opportunity of travelling down to Yorkshire with so pleasant a companion.

M 2

Suiting the action to the word, he dived under the bed and emerged with a travel-stained portmanteau and valise, and, after half-an-hour's frantic exertion, he had packed up his things, dressed himself, and paid his bill.

"Your letters, sir—where are they to be sent ?" inquired the landlady, as he got into the cab.

"Letters ! oh, keep 'em till I return ; and if any one calls, say I have gone up country."

As the young men took train for York, Mr. Magnus, with a severe expression of countenance, ascended with a slow and gouty gait the doorsteps of Joseph's late abode.

It may be supposed that Jack Aventayle's new-born desire for Joseph Manuel's society arose from the young soldier's sudden appreciation of certain sterling qualities that possibly lurked low down beneath the East Indian's unpromising exterior; this, however, was not the case : Aventayle regarded Manuel as the whimsical product of an incomprehensible land. At their first meeting he had recognized that between Joseph's faculties, sentiments, and propensities and his own there was absolutely nothing in common, but after hearing what had passed at the Duchess's dinner-party, it occurred to him that the boredom of country-house life might be relieved by making poor Manuel play Rajah to Lady Helmethame's unconscious guests. With this in view, he had prevailed upon the facile Lilipatian to take his Oriental plumage with him to Yorkshire, and on the evening of their arrival, had duly sent Mr. Abiram a cheque for a handsome figure in payment. Among the guests at Clovenhelm were Lady Louisa Bever and Miss Angelica Magnus, who, with her elder sister, had been invited at the instance of Jack Aventayle, but at the last moment Trelise had caught cold and could not come.

On seeing Miss Magnus at breakfast, Joseph's first impulse was to flee, for he feared that beholding him arrayed in robe and turban, she would expose the impudent deception and would cause his visit to end in obloquy. Jack Aventayle, however, soon lulled his terrors by assuring him that he had already persuaded Miss Magnus, who, unlike the rest of her family, was of a credulous and confiding disposition, that Joseph was in very fact the Rajah of Lilipatam, but that having come to England on a secret mission on behalf of the Indian Government, he had hitherto concealed his identity for purposes of State, and the object of his journey being now attained, the necessity for concealment no longer existed.

The increased respect infused into the young lady's demeanour towards him satisfied Joseph that Aventagle's version had been accepted; and when that politic young gentleman added that Angelica had been expressly cautioned to abstain from all mention of the Rajah in her letters home, as H. H. was taking a little holiday unknown to the Indian authorities, who believed him to be on his way back to his Principality, Joseph once again enjoyed existence. No ephemeral animalcule basking in the sunshine of its single summer-noon lived more thoroughly in the passing hour; he highly appreciated this country-house life—it was so quiet, luxurious, and regular; and he delighted with childlike glee in his gorgeous Indian costume, and in the gleams and flashes of his Brummagem gauds. His vanity, moreover, was gratified by the deference with which he was treated by every one with whom he came in contact. Atavism was asserting itself, and his former humility gave place to pride that soon swelled into arrogance. He began to give himself airs, and the deference accorded to him increased; he grew presumptuous, and respect became homage. As the days passed by without any circumstance of alarm, his early fears of discovery and exposure gradually vanished. His reliance, moreover, in the last resort was on Jack, who, if there should be a scandal, would be involved in it equally with the leading character; and the Honourable Aventayle, as Joseph called him, had influential friends who could protect them both.

Jack Aventayle marked with much amusement Joseph's increasing insolence; the peacock strut, the pompous pose, the supercilious glance, were to Jack the occasion of increasing diversion as the hour of the inevitable downfall approached. Snooseby was within five miles of Clovenhelm, and Jack had learnt from Angelica that the Magnus family were to return to their country quarters in a week's time.

In order that the farce should not be ended prematurely, Aventayle did all in his power to prevent any untimely catastrophe; and when Lady Tymberdale, actuated by a healthy spirit of emulation, ran a Nawab, a genuine article lately imported from Bengal, guaranteed too by the Secretary of State, and proposed to bring the two Eastern kings together, so that the country might be set a-blinking by their combined radiance, Jack, seeing strong barbed wire ahead, earnestly represented to his aunt that their Rajah was a Hindoo and the other fellow, a Mohammedan, between which races there existed so murderous

an antagonism, that if the two potentates, armed
as they were with sword and dagger, were allowed
to meet, the delicate parquet flooring of De Lacey
Court might be stained with royal blood, in which
case, persons without potentates would have an opportunity of making unfriendly and damaging remarks.

Chance threw Lady Louisa and Joseph much
together at Clovenhelm; neither of them rode or
cared for walking, so it fell out that during the
greater part of the day they, among the entire house
party, were the only people that remained at home.
They sat on the terrace, for the weather was
exquisite, or strolled in the gardens and conserva-
tories; but their favourite resort was the palm-house,
where, seated among tropical ferns or under the
drooping vegetation of the cocoa-nut and the fan-
shaped leaves of the palmetto, Lady Louisa discoursed with what to any one but the torpid Joseph
would have been maddening iteration, upon her
darling theme. Indeed, how could she do otherwise
with such harmonious surroundings—palms, tree-
ferns, a rajah, and the thermometer at 85°? Why,
it was a perfect eidolon of the East.

Lady Helmethame, indulging her relative's
humour, had placed her near Joseph at table, and

people began to remark in a half-joking way that her Ladyship and his Highness were becoming uncommonly good friends. Joseph, who, as we have heard his father observe, was no fool, could not long be insensible of the favour in which he was held by the romantic though middle-aged beauty, and soon an incident occurred that inspired him with delirious imaginings.

One evening at dessert they had pulled a cracker together, and the motto part being with Joseph, he was told to read it; but when his eyes fell upon the lines he displayed such confusion and made so clumsy an attempt to excuse himself that Lady Louisa's curiosity was aroused.

"Rajah, I insist on your reading it," said she, laughing at his embarrassment.

"I reely, reely can't," replied the blushing Joseph, with a nervous giggle. "Let's pull another," and he tried to hide the paper under his plate.

"Give that motto to me, Rajah," commanded her Ladyship, with the pretty, spoilt-child imperiousness that had proved so irresistible to the gallants of twenty years ago—"immediately, if you please, sir," and she held out her heavily-ringed hand.

Joseph, with many shifty glances round the

table and murmured protests to his companion, reluctantly complied with the mandate; but to his profound surprise the perusal of the poesy produced no more effect upon the reader than upon the bonbon that it had enclosed. The verse ran thus:—

" Some Phyllis soothes each lover's life ;
No shepherd is without a wife ;
What happiness would be my lot,
If you, dear girl, would share my cot."

"I wonder what sort of people write cracker poetry," she asked, as she unconcernedly handed the paper back to Joseph.

"Men who have failed in the sugar-plum business," replied Jack, who sat on the other side of her. " What was in that motto ? "

" Only some trash about a shepherd's cot," said she.

But as Joseph reflected upon the composure with which the sentiment had been received, his thoughts grew blissfully tempestuous.

" Look at that silver Queen, 'that orbèd maiden with white fire laden, whom mortals call the moon,'" sighed Lady Lousia, as she sat after dinner with Joseph in the niche of the hall window, gazing out on the great park. The full moon rising over the top of the dark wood that formed a distant background was

beginning to turn the park into fairyland, and Joseph
replied that it was " veree elegant indeed."

"It is the gift of the East, that wonderful
mysterious East, wherein lies India, the land of my
longing," continued the lady. " Oh, Rajah! have
we not from that generous quarter everything that
is good ? "

" Yes," assented Joseph; " good tobacco, good
arrack, veree good curry-stuff."

Not attending to his prosaic reply, the poetess
went on : " It is there that the heavenly bodies rise ;
it is thence that the wise men came with their
gifts ; it is from there that we received the nascent
arts and sciences—and more, unspeakably more, than
these."

" All sorts of best supplies," put in Joseph.

"Ah, what does it not supply?" said she. "It gives
us all that adorns our life: gold, silk, pearls, precious
stones ; and while with one hand it dazzles our eyes
with the diamonds of Golcondah, with the other it
delights our palate with the spices of Ceylon. Oh,
beloved and bounteous East, what would I not give
to breathe thine aromatic air, and to repose upon thy
golden sands ! "

As she sat with her hands clasped and her still

beautiful eyes gazing rapturously into space, she looked in the dim light of the hall remarkably handsome. Joseph, partly carried away by the speaker's enthusiasm, and partly impelled by the episode of the cracker, suddenly took the leap that he had for some days past been screwing up his resolution to essay.

"Pardon my imprudence," he gasped, "but I will take you, dear my Lady "—and he regarded her with an amorous ogle intended to be a glance of the tenderest meaning—" I will take you to the sweet and spicee East, if you will honour me by becoming my nuptial wife, and—and sharing my 'umble leetle cot !"

Lady Louisa started, she had never suspected the possibility of this. Joseph appeared to be so staid, so unimpressionable, and already so heavily-wived. It pleased her to indulge in poetic fancies with this Eastern prince; his actual presence in turban and caftan, diamonds and dagger, gave local colour to her sentimental utterances, and enabled her to realize certain favourite passages in *Lallah Rookh* and *The Giaour* in a vivid and satisfactory manner. The Rajah was useful as an ornamental background, or as an object in a lesson; but to marry him !—and the blood rushed to her face as she said with a smile: "And the other poor dears—the queens and sultanas —what would they say?"

"There are no others—you would be the only 'dear,'" blurted Joseph. "What queens and sultanas have I got?"

"Fie!" exclaimed Lady Louisa, holding up her finger reprovingly—"fibs, Rajah, naughty fibs! You confessed to me at the Duchess of Daylesford's that there were a good many ladies in your palace at Lilipatam."

Joseph's face fell; he had altogether forgotten that damaging admission.

Lady Lousia continued: "And, Rajah, I am told that you are a Hindu. Now, if you should unfortunately die before I do, I should have to be burnt alive, you know, like the wives of Arvalan in *The Curse of Kehama* :—

> "' At once on every side
> The circling torches drop,
> At once on every side
> The fragrant oil is poured ;
> At once on every side
> The rapid flames rush up.'

"Now, I don't want to play the part of Azla and Nealliny."

" No, no, you sha'n't be burnt; there is no suttee
now. I will see to it, my dearest madam—I will take
particular care of you."

" But unhappily you would not be in a position to
enforce your commands."

Joseph was silent; what should he do now? He
had learnt from romances and plays how effectually
a proposal of marriage is assisted at the critical
moment by supplicating the treasured object on
bended knee—ought he to kneel at once, or would
it be advisable to delay the playing of this trump
card? Perhaps the lady was already won, and there
was no necessity for risking gymnastic feats unsuited
to corpulent and unelastic people. Had she or had
she not picked up the handkerchief? Her next words
set that question decisively at rest.

" Well, I will not be hard upon you," she laughed—
Joseph rubbed his hands convulsively—" I will not
be too hard upon you, for I consider you have paid
me a very pretty compliment in inviting me to
become a queen; and though I must decline your
extremely flattering offer, please observe, dear Rajah
Manool, that I do so with my warmest thanks. Now,
let us go into the drawing-room, for I am afraid that
after this we can have no more *tête-à-têtes.*"

Joseph, who could have wept with vexation, had no further plea to urge, no new explanation to offer; he was beginning to slide forward on his chair preparatory to plunging on his knees, when Lady Louisa rose and moved towards the drawing-room. The baffled wooer cast a half-languishing, half-spiteful glance at her retreating form, and then, grinding his teeth and sighing deeply, sheepishly followed her across the hall.

On entering the drawing-room he sat down on the nearest vacant chair; it seemed to him as though every one in the room had divined what had passed, and was secretly laughing at his discomfiture, and the idea added gall to the wormwood of his failure.

Near the spot where he had taken refuge sat Miss Angelica Magnus examining a copy of the *Illustrated London News*, in which were delineated various episodes in the Prince of Wales' visit to India. She was looking at a picture of H. R. H.'s reception at a native court in the Doab. Turning to Joseph she asked—

"Is your palace anything like this, Rajah Manool?"

"Like *that!*" he replied pettishly—"oh, no, much larger, very much finer."

" And have you as many elephants ? "

" More, many more. I have also camels, hippopotamuses, bears, rhinoceroses, monkeys, tigers, hunting-leopards—everything."

" You must be very rich ? "

" I am eemmensely rich—I have lacs and lacs of rupees. Nobody in India is richer than I am, and yet people in this country do not value me."

" Rajah," said Lady Helmethame, coming from the piano where she had been playing one of Beethoven's symphonies, " we want you to sing; may I send for your concertina ? "

To the very simplest request made by any one but his hostess Joseph would at that moment have returned a sullen refusal, but he had not quite satisfied himself as to the safety of disobliging Lady Helmethame, so after some demur he ruefully consented to perform.

In the course of a few minutes the sweet singer was seated on an ottoman in the centre of the room surrounded by an admiring circle, to which he droned through his nose, to his own doleful accompanying, *Tha Khataj bai thasi.* As he sang he kept his eyes upon Lady Louisa, and did his utmost to instil a strain of sentimental despair into the words of the song, at the same time endeavouring to heighten the effect by piteous shakes and quavers, wagging his head the while until the feather in his paste aigrette quivered as though in sympathetic pain.

But Lady Louisa was reading the "Light of Asia," and paid no attention to the forlorn looks and melancholy gestures of her sombre swain. His woe-stricken appearance, however, was not lost upon Angelica Magnus, who observed the above-mentioned indications of sensibility with much interest and curiosity, and recalling the Rajah's last words to her, wondered exceedingly why people in England did not appreciate him.

IV.

A few days after the events just recorded, Jack Aventayle drove a coach-load of his aunt's guests to Scarborough for the day.

Lady Louisa being of the party, Joseph, anxious to repair the breach between them, gladly accepted Jack's offer of a seat on the roof.

Our fat friend had picked up enough information about Aventayle's family to be aware that Lady

Louisa, though it pleased her to bewail her inability to afford to travel in India, was an uncommonly rich woman, and it was clear to the astute but sluggish adventurer that he could find no better way of settling himself in life than to hang up his hat, or rather his turban, in Lady Louisa's lobby. He knew that a painful scene would follow the discovery of his deception, but that was a detail with which he was prepared to reckon ; whatever happened, his main object would be secured, namely, the maintenance of Joseph Manuel in some form or other during the term of his natural life. But if this praiseworthy effort for independence was to be made at all, now was the time for action. Joseph had an uneasy sensation that the days of sunshine were rapidly drawing to an end, and that the long drear winter in which there is no harvesting of heiresses was near, very near, at hand.

As Lady Louisa occupied the box-seat, Joseph had no opportunity of conversing with her during the drive, but he determined to attach himself to her on their arrival at Scarborough. Since the scene in the hall she had changed her seat at table, and had restricted her intercourse with Joseph to the ordinary social greetings—the dazzling Orient had lost its charm.

It was high time, so Joseph reflected, that this lovers' quarrel, as he fondly deemed it, should cease; he told himself that he was a man of very distinguished appearance; with a fine figure, a handsome face, and a manner—when he chose to make himself pleasant—that no woman with eyes and ears could long withstand. Yes, Lady Louisa should without further loss of time be whistled back like a stray pigeon to its cote.

But as Fate would have it, when the coach discharged its passengers in the court-yard of the inn, the portly Eastern had so much difficulty in getting down the ladder that when he reached the ground he found every one, except himself and Miss Magnus, paired. Jack, accompanied by Lady Louisa, was busily engaged in seeing to the stabling of his team; and Angelica, looking very forlorn, stood in the archway of the court as though undecided what to do.

" Will you walk with me, Miss Magnus ? " asked Joseph, who despaired of reclaiming Lady Louisa from her cousin. " Ah, please," he added, with his most seductive smile.

Had Joseph come to Scarborough in his royal robes nothing would have induced Angelica to face the curiosity that his appearance in public must have excited; but the Rajah was to-day *incog.*, and no one would turn to gaze at the stout, olive-coloured gentleman in check tweed.

Angelica, however, hesitated; her eyes were fixed somewhat reproachfully upon Jack, who evidently intended to escort his cousin, for he was at that moment ordering a victoria to take them to some distant point of interest.

"Yes," she replied slowly—" yes, Rajah, I will go with you."

She laid a little stress upon the last word, and Joseph, who, in the interpretation of look or accent possessed all the keenness of an Asiatic, was puzzled. Angelica evidently would have preferred to walk with Aventayle. Was she trying to supplant Trelise? Possibly she had done so already, and yet Joseph's quick eye had observed no sign of transferred devotion on the part of the Honourable Jack.

"You seem verce sad, Miss Magnus," began Joseph, in the sort of human purr that he affected when he wished to be particularly tender.

"You were sad the other night," she rejoined.

"Perhaps I had cause; but you," with a sympathetic glance into the girl's sorrowful eyes, "you can have no anxietees?"

"How can you know, Rajah, what my troubles are?"

"She is certainly in love with the Honourable Jack," thought Joseph. "I will try to lead up to the subject."

"What a strange thing love is," said he, "none of us can make any one else love us—isn't it peculiar? Here am I—young, good-looking, rich, royal, and even I cannot make people love me—that is to say, people whose love I want to secure — and you, perhaps, are in the same position?" He uttered the last words in a tone of gentle inquiry, and with a look intended to invite confidence, but which would in a nature more sophisticated than Angelica's have aroused the liveliest suspicion. Angelica was silent, she was debating how far she should unburden her soul to the smooth-spoken gentleman who appeared to be so anxious to console her.

"You also are young, good-looking, and, I think I am right in adding, rich?" murmured Joseph, who, with the volatility of his nature, was beginning to form a new plan of action. "Have I not heard your mother say you have five hundred a year?"

"Oh, no, Rajah. I am not rich; you with your millions must think us all very poor. No, I have only a tiny little three-hundred a year; but it pays for my dresses."

There was another pause, during which Joseph was engaged in mentally converting three hundred pounds into rupees at the current rate of exchange. The silence was broken by Angelica, who resumed :—

"But, Rajah Manool, I can't understand what you mean when you say that you are not appreciated. I should have thought everybody liked you. All your subjects must love you. Surely my father does ? "

"Yes, yes," said Joseph, feeling that he must not indulge in any personal attacks upon Mr. Magnus in this quarter. "A good and noble man is your honourable father—a good and noble man. Yes, he loves me—veree much, like a son, I might even say like a son-in-law; indeed, he once said to me that nothing would give him greater satisfaction than to welcome me in that capacitee into his household."

" He will be so glad to see you, Rajah," returned Angelica; " he often mentioned your name in his letters, and called you an enlightened young ruler."

" When — when does your honourable father return ? " asked Joseph, with a slight tremor in his tone.

" I am sorry to say not for a fortnight; he has

been detained in London by Lord Warberry on a
subject connected, I believe, with Lilipatam; but you,
of course, know all about it." Joseph thought he
could guess the subject of his Lordship's solicitude.
" And," continued Angelica, " Lord Warberry's time
is so taken up with other things that he can't make a
definite appointment till the end of the month, but
may want to see father any day between this and
then; so poor father can't leave London."

They had now crossed the Cliff Bridge and were
about to follow the rest of the party to the South
Bay, but Joseph suddenly proposed that they should
explore the old town, in which pleasant occupation
we will for the present leave them.

"I am so glad you let me take possession of you,
Jack," laughed Lady Louisa, as she and Aventayle
drove out of the inn-yard; " it was so good of you.
I know you wanted to go with one of the girls; but
the truth is, I am beginning to be a little afraid of
your royal friend. I am sure he meant to make
himself my convoy to-day, for as we were driving
down I could see, whenever I turned my head, his
eyes fixed on me in his half-bold, half-obsequious
way. I don't like that man's eyes."

" Oh! he's harmless enough," said Jack contemptuously ; " if he's cheeky to you, hit him on the head with your sunshade, and you'll soon bring him to his bearings."

Joseph and Miss Magnus were late in rejoining the coach. They had each been photographed by a new process, the operation had been long and tedious, and the negatives would take some time to develop— they were to return in a fortnight for the colour- ing.

The journey back was as uneventful as the drive out, but all declared that they had spent a most delightful day.

Time at Clovenholm passed like the days in Lotus- land ; the weather was brilliant, and the heat intense. To Joseph it was always afternoon, for he indulged his constitutional laziness to its fullest extent, and never appeared in public till the luncheon-bell had sounded.

Lunch was over, and Joseph, smoking one of Aventayle's regalias, was lying on the terrace, basking luxuriously in the full blaze of the after- noon sun. And as he lay stretched out at full length upon the easiest of garden-chairs, and watched " with half-dropt eyelid still " the delicate little wreaths of white smoke floating away in the warm air, the picture was suggestive of a pampered bacon-pig that dozes and battens through summer and autumn regardless of the coming of that blue-aproned Nemesis who will knock at the sty-door when the leaves are sere. His complacency increased day by day, and he lived his Satrap life as though it were terminable by death alone.

Yet that very morning he had gazed upon the writing on the wall. The *Tekel, Upharsin* was contained in a letter from Mrs. Magnus to Aventayle, which Jack lost no time in handing to Manuel, remarking as he did so that the game appeared to be about up. There was no doubt that matters had now passed from the bright region of pleasantry into the grim domain of hostile investigation. The part of the letter having interest for Joseph ran thus :—

" What has become of Mr. Manuel ? An inquiry is proceeding at the Feudatory Office at which his presence is absolutely necessary. He left town without giving an address, and my husband, though cruelly disabled by gout, is trying every available means of discovering his whereabouts. It appears that there is a person going about under the title of Rajah of Lilipatam. Can that be Mr. Manuel ?

The Resident declares that if this should prove to be the case he will hand him over to the police as an impostor."

Joseph received this communication with a serene composure that astonished his ally, and it required the exertion of all Jack's influence to induce the bland pretender to agree to leave Clovenhelm on the following day. It was known that Mr. Magnus was to return to Snooseby that evening, and Jack, though willing enough to take part in a practical joke on the largest scale, had no wish to inflict upon his aunt the pain of seeing one of her guests marched off under the charge of the police.

As Joseph had pleaded his inability to leave York-shire without paying his second visit to the Scar-borough photographer, with whom, in fact, the appointment stood for that very day, Aventayle undertook to drive him over on his drag that after-noon, and at once went off to make up a party; leaving Joseph, dreamily enjoying the genial sun-shine and lazily smoking his claro, to await the arrival of the coach.

The party was composed of the same people, excepting Lady Louisa who had returned to London, as on the last occasion ; and on arriving at Scarborough, Miss Magnus and Joseph having business at the photographer's walked away together; they, however, brought home no proofs of the pictures, the process having proved to be longer than had been anticipated even by the artist.

That evening the entire house-party at Clovenhelm drove five miles to a grand ball given in honour of the Rajah of Lilipatam by a Mrs. Cleophas W. Mends. This lady was a fabulously rich American widow, who had recently taken one of the finest places in the North Riding, and with transatlantic grace and adroitness had with the least practicable delay vaulted into the front rank of county society.

" They tell me you are to have quite a royal reception, Maharajah." Joseph had that morning promoted himself a degree in rank. " I hope it will not annoy you," said Lady Helmethame, as they drove up Mrs. Mends' avenue, " but you are, of course, accustomed to that sort of thing."

Joseph was silent; when he was puzzled he held his peace. In a few minutes more they entered the gravel sweep leading to the door. The garden looked like fairyland; the trees were crowded with Chinese lanterns. From dark corners magnificent fireworks threw out showers of variegated sparks. Coloured lights were cast on the fountains, and a large transparency depicted Joseph Manuel mounted on a fiery charger leading his forces to battle.

As the carriage drew up under the portico, a stentorian voice shouted the command—

" Present arms ! "

Then a drum began to roll, and a fife band broke into some martial strain.

" The volunteers," explained Lady Helmethame.

On descending from the carriage, Joseph beheld some hundred men in military uniform drawn up two deep on each side of the door, the privates presenting arms and the officers saluting. Joseph acknowledged the compliment by a low salaam, and offering his arm to Lady Helmethame, mounted the steps with great majesty.

When the guest of the evening entered the ballroom, the dancing ceased, the assembly forming a lane through which Joseph, following a gentleman of very dignified deportment, who had been specially selected for the occasion, proceeded to the end of a room, where a daïs covered with red cloth had been prepared for him; the centre of the daïs was occupied by a magnificent throne composed of gilded wood-work and purple velvet cushions. While he paced up the hall, every nerve in his large body vibrating deliciously with a fool's vainglory, the band thundered out the "Rajah's March," a piece that had been composed for the occasion by the band-master. As he passed in his haughty progress up the large room, the ladies courtesied and the men bowed with becoming reverence.

On the daïs stood Mrs. Cleophas W. Mends, who, taking the "Rajah's" hand in both her own, effusively welcomed him to her "poor abode."

When Joseph was satisfactorily installed, Mrs. Mends sat down on a low chair by the side of the throne, and dancing recommenced. After the dance, people were brought up and presented to H.H. Rajah Manool, after which dancing was resumed; then followed more presentations, and after about an hour of this the hostess led her regal guest into a charming little boudoir, arranged in green and gold, where supper had been laid exclusively for him, as though he were the Prince of Wales. Then back to the ball-room, and again to the boudoir, and yet again to the boudoir, and again, for Joseph, with sorrow be it recorded, was growing very swinish, and not only ate, but drank more than was good for him.

"You will think it peculiar, Rajah," simpered his

hostess, as they sat on the daïs regarding the gay throng circling before them—" very peculiar I am sure, that an American should feel so greatly honoured by your presence in her house ; for we States people, you know, profess to despise crowns and sceptres. But I tell you, sir, I love them ; I do not scruple to confess that I would gladly wear a crown myself if I had the right."

Joseph thought it was a pity he had not met this lady at an earlier period of his brief career, but he merely bowed and observed: " Some one has said, Ma'am, ' the head that lies, uneasy wears the crown.' "

" Yes, sir, I think I have heard that before. Do you know the Queen of England ? "

" Well, no, not intimately."

" I suppose, now, she does not possess half the power over her subjects that you do over yours ? You, for instance, could order a woman to be tied up in a sack and thrown into the sea ? "

" Oh, yes, I could do that easily."

" Or have a man stamped on by an elephant ? "

" Oh dear, yes; or burnt or skinned alive," replied the audacious impostor, who had discovered that the interest which he excited was heightened by the occasional suggestion that he had power to commit hideous barbarities.

"Really now! And is every one in your State, white or black, obliged to obey you?"

"I should rather think so," said the unblushing Joseph; "not a European in *my* country dare shake a finger at me. Why, I should have his head off in no time."

At this moment an elderly gentleman entered the ball-room, and, approaching the daïs, stood with eyes blazing with wrath and indignation in front of the puppet king. Never before had so fierce a light beaten round a throne, yet the occupant of the gilt and velvet structure of Mrs. Mends appeared utterly unaware of the radiance that was being shed upon him.

The wrathful old gentleman seemed to be somewhat infirm, for one hand rested upon a stick and the other was supported by the arm of a young lady. After regarding Joseph scorchingly for a moment or two, the new-comer drew forth a pair of gold pince-nez glasses, and, carefully adjusting them, stared at Mrs. Mends' royal guest with increasing combustion.

"That person appears to be acquainted with you,

Rajah," said Mrs. Mends—she had seen some rough work in the West, and read mischief in the stranger's eye. " Do you know him ? "

" Yes," replied Joseph, who from the first had recognized Mr. Magnus and Trelise, " his name is Lemuel Magnus; he was once Resident at my court, but he went mad, and I had to dismiss him. He believes that my father, the late Rajah, is still alive, and that I have no right to the throne. He will, perhaps, be abusive, but you have servants, dear madam, who can turn him out."

Whether it was to be ascribed to the good cheer of the boudoir or to some other cause that this history has not yet elucidated, Joseph Manuel maintained a perfect composure, and met the Resident's angry eyes with a stolid equanimity that for one in Joseph's peculiar position was perhaps the best defence that could be adopted.

Mr. Magnus having completed his survey, nodded his head emphatically to his companion, and with a terrible expression of countenance proceeded to mount the daïs. Planting himself in front of the throne where Joseph sat gleaming in paste and tinsel, he bent forward like a fighting-cock about to strike, and in his most rasping growl ejaculated—" Mountebank ! "

Joseph took no heed of this flattering salutation, but calmly continued his conversation with Mrs. Mends.

Mr. Magnus' face flushed a fine ruthenean red; he struck his stick violently on the floor in order to command attention, and in a louder and more strident key exclaimed, with a sharp rap of his stick on the ground between each word—

" Charlatan, look me in the face! "

But Manuel maintained his conversation with the lady by his side as unconcernedly as though Mr. Magnus were a slave of the palace repeating some trite formula of Eastern adulation.

Stung to fury by this studied contempt on the part of the wretch whom he had come to pull down and pulverize, Mr. Magnus grasped Joseph's velvet sleeve and bellowed in his ear—

" Despicable hound! you *shall* hear me!—you shall—you shall—you shall! " and with each " shall " the speaker gave a fierce tug at his intended victim's arm.

Finding that he could no longer ignore the Resident, Joseph calmly turned his head, and haughtily twisting his moustache with his disengaged hand—a close observer might have noticed a slight trembling of the fingers—addressed Mr. Magnus in Hindu-stani. The Resident understood that language perfectly, but he was determined that the dialogue should be conducted in a tongue that all present could understand.

"Aha! you miserable swindler, so you desire a private interview at my house to-morrow, do you? To prevent a scandal, eh? No, sir, no! what has to be said shall be said here, and in English, before all these ladies and gentlemen—whom you insult by your presence among them. Now, mumming rogue and jackanapes, what have you to say for yourself?"

Joseph smiled sadly at his hostess, who replied by an intelligent nod.

"Infamous impostor! remove that frippery and leave this house!" panted Mr. Magnus, his words struggling with one another in the frenzy of his denunciation. "You, you, *you* on a throne!—abject, crawling cheat! don't I know you, and your whole family!—don't I know your father?"

Again Joseph smiled mournfully at Mrs. Mends, who glanced significantly at the fast-assembling crowd and tapped her forehead with her finger.

"Will you come off that throne, you usurping

r-r-rascal ? " roared Mr. Magnus, now almost beside
himself at Joseph's calm indifference. "Listen to
me," he vociferated, turning to the crowd, "that
pitiful humbug there is no more a Rajah than I am;
his father lives at Lilipatam and is——"

By this time Joseph had risen from his regal chair,
and was standing by the speaker's side. "Listen to
me, Mr. Magnus, before you say what perhaps you
will to-morrow wish unsaid."

Joseph spoke so impressively that Mr. Magnus
paused in his harangue, and glared in wonder at the
bold adventurer. Before the Resident had recovered
from his surprise, Joseph had added a few, a very few,
words in a low tone ; the whispered accents reached
no ear save that for which they were intended, and
upon the owner of that ear the effect was potent
indeed.

As he listened, Mr. Magnus trembled violently,
then he began to rock a little on his feet as though
he would fall from the daïs, but when the speaker
concluded, the Resident drew his arm from that of
his daughter, straightened himself by a mighty effort,
grasped his stick in both hands, and dealt such a
blow on Joseph Manuel's head that had not
Abiram's turban been closely and heavily wadded,

society would have had to deplore the loss of its latest lion. As it was, the stroke brought Manuel to his knees, and he might have fallen further had not a dozen hands, outstretched at Mrs. Mends' agonized entreaty to " save the Rajah," caught him as he sank.

The injured man having been carried with exceeding care into the boudoir, and there tenderly laid upon a couch, an eminent surgeon, who providentially was among the guests, after a long and minute examination pronounced His Highness to have sustained no injury whatever, and the cheering report was rapidly circulated among the anxious assembly. But in spite of the reassuring diagnosis, Joseph was not permitted by his hostess to go home immediately, as he fervently desired, but was detained upon the sofa for the space of an hour told by the ormolu clock on the mantelpiece ; during which period Mrs. Cleophas W. Mends, assisted by the three prettiest women in the room, alternately fanned the patient's broad face and bathed his temples with eau-de-Cologne ; dry champagne being administered internally at five-minute intervals.

As Mr. Magnus, now in the foaming and inarticulate stage of mental tempest, was by turns led, pushed, and carried to his conveyance, Joseph, petted by beauty and surrounded by luxury, lay sipping the choicest brand of Widow Clicquot, and smiling as he heard the thunders of his late assailant growing fainter in the distance.

It was the culmination of the rocket.

The next morning Joseph Manuel, pleading a pressing summons from Lord Warberry, returned by the earliest train to London, and a carriage came to Clovenhelm to convey Miss Angelica Magnus to Pillula Cottage, the rural abode of her family.

On arriving at the cottage, which lay within an easy drive of Lady Helmethame's, Angelica was summoned to her father's private room.

Both Mr. and Mrs. Magnus were present, and each presented a sufficiently awe-inspiring appearance.

For a moment there was a petrifying silence, then Mr. Magnus spoke.

" Is it true ? "

" W—w—what ? " stammered Angelica, turning very pale and cold, for she knew what her father meant.

" That you were married to that black scoundrel at a registrar's office in Scarborough yesterday afternoon ? "

" I married the Mahara—a—a—a—jah," sobbed Angelica.

"The Maharajah!" shouted Mr. Magnus, with infinite scorn. "The Maharajah, forsooth! You know he's no Rajah, but a poor, mean, pitiful jerry-sneak of an apothecary's son—you shameless minx!"

"Leave her to me, Lemuel," interposed Mrs. Magnus, who saw that her husband was on the verge of madness, and, unless checked, might say things that would upset his daughter utterly.

At this juncture a servant knocked at the door and announced Mr. Aventayle " for Mr. Magnus alone."

The congress was thereupon hastily prorogued, Mrs. Magnus leading the tearful Angelica to her own room for a quiet talk, and possibly a little sympathetic weeping too, while Mr. Magnus cleared his brow and endeavoured to summon the gracious smile with which he received choice and valued visitors.

The conference was brief, and when the door had closed upon the caller, Mr. Magnus rang his bell with a force sufficient almost to tear it from the wall.

"Send your mistress to me," shouted he hoarsely

to the scared maid-servant, who afterwards declared in full kitchen that if this sort of thing went on she must either give warning or die of spangles in the heart.

"Marian," he groaned, as his wife hurriedly entered the room, " young Aventayle came over to propose for——"

" Trelise ? " gasped Mrs. Magnus, casting up her eyes in pious gratitude. " Heaven be thanked ! "

"No—for Angelica," said Mr. Magnus, administering a kick to the footstool that drove it through the window.

*   *   *   *

When Angelica became aware of the deception to which she had fallen a victim, she declared, and she adhered to the decision, that nothing on earth should induce her to link her life to that of such a shameless impostor.

Joseph, however, showed unexpected determination, and, stimulated and supported by a low firm of attorneys, threatened legal proceedings. Mr. Magnus, on his side, talked of a criminal prosecution, upon which Joseph snapped his fingers and pointed to the effects of the *exposé* upon Miss Angelica, and in the end the quarrel drifted into a compromise ;

the terms of which were that Joseph should hold his tongue about the marriage, and should abandon all claim to his wife, in consideration of receiving two-thirds of her income, namely, £200 a year, to be duly paid and delivered to him quarterly in India.

When last heard of he was living with his father and mother on the Plaintain Hills, where he was doing something in coffee; he had grown enormously stout, and had become so confirmed a toper that his death might be expected at any moment. When he was overcome by his potations, it was his custom to twine a napkin round his head and sit upon the table, insisting upon all present saluting him under the style and title of His Majesty the Maharajah of Asia.

Mr. Magnus "retired," shorn of his adventitious attributes and reduced to his natural dimensions, occupies a minor position in county society; he has grown moody and splenetic, and his friends observe that his testiness increases should the conversation turn upon Eastern subjects, that his humour becomes actively morose should reference be made to an Eastern potentate, but that he becomes absolutely unmanageable should any stranger be so ill-advised as to mention in his hearing the apparently innocent appellative—Maharajah.

SHAMEFUL BEHAVIOUR

SOME men blamed the Major, others condemned the Captain, but all the women were down upon Polly Reynard. They said she had behaved "shamefully," with a strong accent on the "shame." For my part, I offer no opinion on the matter, I merely relate the facts as they occurred.

Lovelace Grey was as devil-may-care a Captain of Horse as could be found in the wildest cavalry regiment in Europe. His manners were engaging, and his face was handsome, but alas! his morals were bad. This young officer's career, up to the date when our tale begins, may be described in a few words. A peer's son, and the heir to a fine fortune, he was naturally sent to Eton, whose classic and humid precincts he abandoned, after the customary noviciate, for the more congenial surroundings of White's and the Guards' Club. About this period of his life his name for the first time figured in the

reports of Doctors' Commons, where he suffered
heavy amercement at the hands of a married jury
and a draconic judge. Having in the space of
eighteen months run through most of his money,
he found it convenient, with a view to squander
the remainder more at leisure, to bid farewell
to the *corps d'élite*, and accordingly exchanged into
a cavalry regiment of the line. A few weeks
after his transfer he appeared for a second time as
a leading character in the court for the disposal of matrimonial causes, and on this occasion,
the particulars being less to his credit than
were those even of his previous escapade, the
damages were proportionately rigorous. From this
epoch he so arranged his life that the Queen's
Proctor knew him no more, for the expenses attending upon this last event had exhausted what
remained to him of unearned increment arising from
mortgages and post-obits. After a brief but
terrifically rapid career in the 3rd Light Spears,
Grey found himself obliged by the ever-increasing
pressure of debt to exchange into the 4th Heavy
Sabres, then under orders for India. The Sabres, in
the ordinary course of relief, found their way to
Drumgalore, where the 60th Native Infantry were in

garrison ; and this brings us to Polly Reynard, and opens our tale.

Major and Mrs. Reynard were at breakfast. The English mail had arrived that morning, and an overland letter addressed to Major Reynard, 60th N. I., lay open on the table. The Major played gloomily with the missive, while his wife spread anchovy paste on slender slices of toast and placed them invitingly before him. When the Major was upset, he proclaimed a personal fast, and on such occasions his wife would save him from starvation by luring him with dainty particles, as though he were a canary. The Major, be it known, was a confirmed invalid, prematurely broken down by the Indian climate and grievously harassed by an immovable incubus of debt. Hope had long been a stranger to his languid heart, and it was evident that under the combined influence of an enlarged liver and an attenuated balance-sheet, he was slowly, but surely drifting to the station cemetery. He just managed to struggle through the work that the day brought forth ; but like a worn-out old boot which is always being sent to the cobbler, he was hardly ever out of the hands of the regimental doctor. The doctor, who was weary of vamping and

welting this perpetual patient, would long ago
have sent him on medical certificate to England,
had it not been well known to every one that the
unfortunate man would have found it impossible
to raise the money required for the journey, if
indeed a legion of alert and avid creditors would have
allowed him to leave the country.   Such was the
Major.

Mrs. Reynard was a being of a widely different
type; beauty and never-failing health, together with
a buoyant heart and a fund of mother-wit that
Talleyrand himself might have envied, rendered her
at once the most delightful of companions, the most
lovable of wives, and the keenest of domestic
administrators.

Husband and wife were discussing the letter that
lay on the table between them; it was from Mrs.
Reynard's father, an opulent Yorkshire squire.

" I expected nothing more, Polly," sighed the
Major; " he offers me the very thing that I can't
take advantage of, and he knows it."

" Oh, Dick! "

" Well, if he doesn't know it, he ought to.   Everybody knows that I can't leave the country."

" Nothing's impossible, Dick; and if we could get

away, there's an end to all our trouble. You were always well in England. You will have peace of mind, plenty of riding and shooting, and no more guard-duty and parades. Yorkshire, too, is your favourite county, Dickums."

"Aye," replied the Major, with a groan; "but how are we to *get* to Yorkshire? I might as well try to fly to the moon."

"Leave it to me, Dicky boy, and see if I don't manage it somehow or other," and his angel on the hearth shed upon him the cloud-dispelling sunshine of her sweetest smile. It may be stated that Mrs. Reynard had at that moment no more idea how the feat was to be accomplished than she had of squaring the circle or of satisfying her husband's creditors, but, like Napoleon, she refused to admit that anything was impossible. The letter under consideration was a reply to the last of a long series of appeals for subsidies, which the Major ever since the time of his marriage, seven years before, had periodically addressed to his father-in-law. At first Mr. Baxterly had assisted his daughter's husband in a sufficiently liberal manner, but as the step-debts and the compound interest on the money-lender's bills accumulated, the Squire's generosity waned, and he had at last announced his ultimatum. The Major must straightway leave the army and go home, where he would be appointed land-steward of the Baxterly estates; he and his wife were to live at the Abbey with the Squire, at whose death Mrs. Reynard would receive a very liberal settlement. But the Squire's munificence had its limits; the letter said nothing as to the means by which the ensnared warrior was to escape from the land of bondage.

That night there was a large ball at the Sabres' mess. The Cavalry always gave *the* ball of the season, and the dance in question promised to eclipse all its predecessors. Mrs. Reynard and her husband were of course among the guests. It was an article of that admirable woman's creed that her " Dicky boy " should be present at every scene of gaiety garrison life afforded. " It did him good," she said. In point of fact, the poor man on these occasions suffered, both in mind and body, more acutely than ever; but his wife, who was the soul of every social gathering, most thoroughly enjoyed herself, and never failed to absorb stores of happiness, which, after the manner of certain lustrous gems, she assimilated and carried away with her, diffusing the hived radiance upon her poverty-darkened home.

The mess-house was superbly decorated ; the walls glowed with flowers and gleamed with burnished weapons and accoutrements; the rooms were brilliant with smart frocks and gay uniforms, and many a dainty little arbour, cunningly wrought with lattice-work and greenery, tempted the tired dancers to snatch a few moments' rest free from the glare of lamp and candle.

On the arrival of the Reynards, all the men who happened to be standing near the entrance gathered round the lady, and gleefully booked her for as many dances as the laughing beauty deigned to bestow, after which she was whirled away by one of them, and her husband saw but little of her till the time arrived for going home. As for him, he spent the intervening hours drooping in doorways or propping himself against walls; sometimes he would drift into a seat among the chaperones, or would gloomily nibble a biscuit in company with some other stiff limbed senior who was owned by a dancing wife.

Chief among Mrs. Reynard's army of admirers was Captain Grey, and this evening he had succeeded in securing her for the first two round dances, all the supper waltzes, and an extra. He had a great deal to

say to her, and he certainly made the most of these not
inconsiderable opportunities.   His conversation, I
am bound to record, bore upon his hopeless adoration
of his bewitching partner.

> " He spoke of love [not] such as spirits feel
>   In worlds whose course is equable and pure."

He moaned through his moustache a prose lyric of
weary longing—he described his joyless heart upon
which her beauty rose like some pure star upon a lonely
mere, and he spoke of the present moment as the turning point of his life, vowing that it rested with her
whether he chose the upward or the downward path.
She was wrong to let him go on, I hear my gentlest
reader say; she could not have been a *really* nice woman.
Madam, did you ever observe the peculiar quality with
which nature has endowed the back of the wild-duck—
a property admirably adapted for the rejection and
extrusion of water ?   Even so was the mind of Mrs.
Reynard in its relation to flattery.   Flattery !—she
had been immersed to the eyes in it ever since she
was a child.   Her father never spoke of her but as
his Hebe or his Iris, and all his hunting friends
readily admitted that she was lovelier than any goddess
in the heathen Pantheon.   She had received nearly

twenty proposals from eligible persons, to say nothing
of the raving of detrimentals, before, with the sweet
inconsequence of womankind, she committed the
first and only blunder of her life, and threw herself
away upon the dismal invalid whom she continued
to love as dearly as husband was ever loved by
wife ; while from the moment of her arrival at
Drumgalore, incense of such subtile flavour had been
burnt upon her altar, and hymns of such fervid
import had been chanted at her shrine, as would
have turned the heads of a London beauty in her
third season, but which this bright, sensible, winning
young person shook off like a grey mallard scattering
water from his crest after a dive.

"But I mean it," whispered Captain Grey, with, for
him, an unusual air of earnestness. Mrs. Reynard,
leaning upon his arm, had paused in an ante-room
to admire a trophy of arms. "I swear I do, Mrs.
Reynard." So well did she keep the men in hand,
that even Grey dared not call her Polly.

"I will think it over," she whispered, as they moved
into the dancing-room.

Some ten days after this episode the post brought
another letter to the Reynards' breakfast-table.
This time it was for the lady, who, after skimming

P

its contents, put it carelessly in her pocket without
showing it to her languid lord.   After breakfast she
went into her bedroom, and sitting on a low chair
by the window, again perused the missive.   Her
eyes continued fixed upon the paper, while her brow
became clouded and her lower lip was pressed between
her teeth.   She read the lines again and again ;
she was evidently sorely perplexed.   At last, something like a tear, an unusual visitant, stole into
her lively eyes and trickled down her cheek.   It was
followed by another and another, and this went on
for five minutes or so.   Suddenly a change came over
her, the shadow vanished from her face, the moisture
was brushed from her lashes, her lip released from its
ivory vice again formed itself into a smile, and,
crushing the paper firmly in her hand, she sprang to
her feet, a heroine prepared for all emergencies.
The letter ran thus :—

                    " Madras Club, *Dec.* ——
" Dear Mrs. Reynard,
        " I was dining last night with an old chum of
mine, an attorney here, who told me that a writ
was out to arrest the Major at the suit of Gohlum
Doss, the money-lender, and that a High Court

bailiff—a European—would start at once for Drumgalore : so Reynard had better look out.

"Yours always very sincerely,

"CHARLES FAIRFIELD.

"P.S.—My friend says *they can't enter your house if
you keep the doors locked.*"

Fairfield was a subaltern in the Major's regiment,
and, like all other boys in the station, was Mrs.
Reynard's sworn bond-slave. Charlie, before going
on leave, had been strictly enjoined to discover what
this particular money-lender was about, for the man,
who was one of poor Reynard's heaviest creditors,
had recently displayed ominous signs of angry im-
patience. The first thing to be done, said Mrs.
Reynard to herself as she put on her sun-hat, is to
have Dick placed on the sick-list. There was
no difficulty in accomplishing this, the doctor's only
anxiety regarding his patient arose when he had to
pronounce him fit for duty. The Major had now
been more than three months out of the doctor's
hands, and it was but natural that the convalescent
should suffer from the effects of such prolonged
activity.

Whenever Reynard was on the sick-list, his wife

undertook the task of exercising his charger—the solitary occupant of his stable. So the morning after the doctor had reported her husband unfit for duty, Polly cantered slowly down the Madras Road revolving many things in her fertile mind. When Mrs. Reynard went out riding there was never any lack of cavaliers in her train ; all the horses and ponies in the place were as friendly with Mrs. Reynard's inexpensive mount as the riders were with its mistress ; but from this day forth she shunned the path of the riders, and every morning and evening patrolled the quiet and secluded road leading to the Presidency town. One friend alone had been made aware of her new haunt, and on these occasions, unless stables or some other duty intervened, Captain Grey was seldom absent from her side.

I may state the fact, though it may not be accepted, that Grey, in spite of his long contact with the gayest portion of the gay world, had still a weak point in his case-hardened heart, and was as deeply in love with Polly Reynard as was the last-joined boy from the depôt. It may be stated that all who came to the station caught the epidemic more or less severely, the intensity of the attack being generally in inverse proportion to the sufferer's age.

At this stage of the story it becomes necessary to explain Captain Grey's intention with regard to our heroine. On the night of the ball he had deliberately proposed that she should run away with him to England, and after being divorced from her poor broken-down husband should become the Honourable Mrs. Grey, and live happily—oh! so happily—ever after; to which enterprising and comprehensive project the lady had so far consented as to vouchsafe it her consideration. Upon which the Captain, gleefully reflecting that the woman who considers is lost, at once wrote to his agents telling them to remit him a large sum of money, and then quietly made his arrangements for leaving the station. They had since the ball spoken many times upon the momentous subject, and Mrs. Reynard had at length brought herself to ask for a fuller exposition of her adorer's plans.

In those days the railway, though it was under rapid construction, had not reached the cantonment of Drumgalore, and the nearest station was still thirty miles off. This distance the Captain proposed to get over at night in his dog-cart, posting a horse halfway. Then the train was to be taken to Bombay, and affairs were to be so arranged that their arrival

at that port would fit in with the departure of the
mail steamer for Brindisi. Mrs. Reynard promised
to think over the scheme, and to give its ingenious
author a definite reply as soon as she was able
to come to a conclusion. Thus matters rested
until the arrival of Fairfield's letter, when the lady
advanced the negociations by consenting to the
elopement under certain definite conditions, one of
which was that the passage should be secured in the
name of Major and Mrs. Reynard; she could not
bear to think of travelling under a false name—"it
was so like a criminal, you know;" the other stipula-
tion being that the ticket should be lodged in her own
hands. The smitten Captain, although he protested
against the latter article as reflecting upon his own
faith, nevertheless readily agreed to the terms.

As she rode one morning to her usual exercise
ground, Mrs. Reynard saw Captain Grey waiting,
according to the custom, at the top of the avenue.
As she approached, he rose in his stirrups and waved
a letter in the air. It was the passage-ticket. The
envelope, though it came enclosed in a letter to
Captain Grey, was addressed to Major Reynard,
60th N. I.

As she placed the precious document carefully in

her saddle-pocket, Mrs. Reynard told Captain Grey with a faltering voice that she was henceforward in his hands.

The delighted warrior proposed to leave Drumgalore that very night; his dog-cart should be at her compound-gate at ten o'clock; they would take the early train to Bombay, and would be in time to catch the next homeward-bound steamer.

This was hurrying matters to a crisis far more rapidly than Mrs. Reynard had contemplate1, and a plea for delay was rising to her lips, when she saw coming down the road that which she had for the last seven days strained her eyes night and morning to discover—Dick's peril.

A tall, heavily-built man, keen-eyed and grey-bearded, with a cheroot in his mouth and a stout bamboo in his hand, was plodding along in the direction of Drumgalore. He was followed by a country-cart, in which apparently he had slept, for it contained, in addition to sundry articles of luggage, a mattress and pillow. As the riders passed him he scanned the Captain's face with much curiosity, while Mrs. Reynard's eyes were riveted with an equal eagerness upon his own. Instinct told her that this was the man who was coming to arrest her husband.

"I think we have gone far enough," she said, turning to her companion. " I am tired this morning, I passed such a wretched night."

As she spoke she took the Captain's letter from her pocket and again read the address—"Major Reynard, 60th N. I." She slipped the ticket into her glove, and playing carelessly with the cover, managed to let it fall full in front of the pedestrian as they passed him on their return The stranger at once picked up the envelope, and, having read it, quickened his pace and called after Grey. " Here, sir, you've dropped something." Grey turned his head.

" It's only an empty envelope that I threw away," said Polly, with an air of unconcern. " Come along, the sun is getting hot."

The man pulled out a bulky pocket-book, and began fumbling among its contents.

"Stop, sir, I want to speak to you," he cried, as he extracted a small piece of paper.

"Lovelace," said Mrs. Reynard hurriedly, seeing that Grey was about to pull up, " I shall be ready at ten o'clock to-night; only promise me to bring your dog-cart to the door, for I can't walk to the gate in the dark," and as she spoke she put her horse into a canter.

Captain Grey, in the whirl of delight into which these words had plunged him, at once lost all thought of the stranger, and setting spurs to his horse, galloped after the lady.

The intelligent reader will already have divined the bearing of Mrs. Reynard's plan. Like many a a high measure of statesmanship, it was remarkable for its simplicity. Her intention was nothing less than to make Captain Grey pay for her husband's escape. " He would have deceived Dick," she argued, " why should I not deceive *him ?* " Matters were now in fair train, and it remained only to eliminate the Captain from the arrangement to ensure complete success. Mrs. Reynard's first idea was to have Grey seized that evening and confined by some of her young friends in the 60th, who would mount guard over him till the morning, by which time she and her husband would be in safety. She had no fear of the consequences to her allies, she felt that she could rely upon the Captain's prudence for their full indemnity.

Affairs had, however, now assumed a new phase, and she decided that her admirer should be removed by the more constitutional method of arrest on civil process. Accordingly when she reached home she communicated to her husband as much of her intentions as she deemed necessary and prudent, and during the remainder of the day she employed herself in making preparations for their journey. Among these preliminaries was the composition and despatch of a short anonymous note to the bailiff, who she accurately divined would be putting up at the rest-house, the usual place of residence for travelling Europeans. The note informed him that Major Reynard of the 60th Regiment would leave his house in a dog-cart at ten o'clock that night for the Tara Railway Station. The missive was signed " A friend of the law."

When the appointed hour rang out from the main-guard, Mrs. Reynard, dressed in a plain serge travelling dress, stood with glittering eyes and a palpitating heart under the porch of her verandah. She had left Reynard waiting in the dining-room, and had assured him with many kisses that she would come back for him in two minutes. The sound of wheels stealthily approaching told her that her lover was true to time, and she felt sure that the tryst would be equally well kept by the bailiff. Grey drew up under the porch and, whispering some loving words suitable to the occasion, told her to give

him her hand and jump up. Putting her foot upon
the wheel, she seized his proffered hand and climbed
lightly to his side. He tried to kiss her, but she
found it necessary at that moment to stoop for her
handkerchief, and, as the horse was restive, the gallant
warrior was obliged to start without that enchanting
stirrup-cup.

As they passed out of the compound-gate Mrs.
Reynard looked keenly around her for the bailiff.
The moon shone brightly and every little bush and
stone was discernible, but the tipstaff was not there.
Misery!—not a soul was to be seen. As she realized
her position a chilling horror gripped her heart, and
she laid her trembling hand upon the Captain's arm.

"Oh! stop—stop for just one little minute! I
have—forgotten my jewel-case."

"Never mind your jewel-case," said Grey, flicking
his horse into a canter; " I will give you heaps and
heaps of jewels, darling."

Mrs. Reynard's nerves were of the purest temper,
her brain was of the clearest, and her heart was
as stout as Bayard's; yet it must be admitted that
for a moment this unexpected turn of events nearly
overwhelmed her. As she was hurried through the
now deserted station she saw more and more clearly

the hideousness of her peril ; every yard they covered diminished her chance of escape, and the first shock nearly caused her to faint outright, but the cool night-air rushing past her temples soon revived her, and she gallantly endeavoured to collect her scattered thoughts. That she would never leave the railway station in Captain Grey's companionship she was firmly resolved, but thoughts of his indignation at her change of mind, of the possibility of his carrying her into the train against her will, of the terrible scandal that must in any case ensue, and, last though not least, of the complete failure of her carefully arranged plans, coupled with the sudden conviction that the bailiff had by some occult skill fathomed her intentions and was even then laying his heavy hand upon poor Dick Reynard's feeble arm, nearly drove her frantic with terror and despair.

" I have arranged everything capitally," said her companion, in a satisfied tone. " The Brigadier made no difficulty about my leave, and Gus Trevellian has taken all my horses. Shall we go by Paris or Vienna ? What a topping good time we'll have ! Can you see what that is just ahead of us ? Is it a bullock-cart ? Heigh ! heigh ! clear the road there," he shouted ; but as the cart remained obstinately fixed in its position, he had to slacken his breakneck pace, and was at length obliged, though most unwillingly, to draw up. The cart with its bullocks was standing right across the road, which it completely blocked.

" The driver is either drunk or asleep," muttered the Captain; " catch hold of the reins for a moment, dear, while I get down and wake him up ; " and, as he had sent his syce in advance, so that they might travel the more lightly, he leaped down to clear the road himself.

At that moment a tall man approached from beneath the shadow of a banyan-tree, and, touching the astonished Captain's shoulder, growled: " I arrest you, Major Reynard, at the suit of Soucar Gohlum Doss, on a High Court warrant."

" Go to the d——l! " shouted the Captain angrily, disengaging his shoulder from the bailiff's finger. " I am not Major Reynard—you have got hold of the wrong man."

" So they *all* says," replied the bailiff imperturbably, adding, " I know you well enough, I see you a-riding along this very road only this morning."

" I am Captain Grey of the 4th Sabres," said

that officer haughtily, " and you touch me at your peril."

" If you be Captain Grey, what be you a-doing with Major Reynard's letters ? " said the man knowingly, at the same time holding up the envelope that Mrs. Reynard had dropped in the morning.

" Ask this lady who I am, if you won't believe me," said the Captain, in desperation, for he began to perceive that this most unfortunate encounter was imperilling his enterprise.

" Who might you be, ma'am ? " inquired the man, looking at Mrs. Reynard.

" I am Mrs. Reynard " replied that lady demurely.

" Ha, ha ! " laughed the bailiff, turning towards Grey, " if you ain't the Major, what be you a-doing along o' his wife ? You're the man, right enough. Ah ! would you ? "

The last exclamation was evoked by the Captain's making a sudden spring for the dog-cart, but the experienced officer of the law had for the last minute or so been fully prepared for that movement, and in the twinkling of an eye he had caught the Captain by the collar and had laid him full length upon the ground.

Mrs. Reynard's opportunity had now arrived. Swiftly turning the horse's head, she drove at full speed back to the cantonment. She found her husband anxiously pacing the verandah.

" You've been a precious long two minutes, Polly," he said, looking at his battered old silver hunter, "nearer half-an-hour, my girl."

Reserving all explanation for a more convenient opportunity, Mrs. Reynard ordered the servants to place the luggage in the dog-cart, and paying them their wages, wrapped her husband up in a tweed shawl and helped him into the vehicle. The Major made no inquiry as to the ownership of the turn-out—any man in the place would have been proud to put the best thing in his stable at Polly's disposal—and as to the main arrangement, *that*, it had been agreed, was to remain a secret until they were on board ship.

In less than ten minutes they were clear of Drumgalore, and were bowling merrily along the road to the railway-station. When they had proceeded about three miles they flew past a bullock-cart that was pursuing its sluggish course in the same direction. A tall man walked behind it chuckling softly to himself, while from the inside depths could be discerned the fierce glow of a cheroot that was evidently being smoked by some one under the influence of strong emotion. Thanks to the second horse so thoughtfully posted by Captain Grey, they were just in time to catch the mail-train to Bombay, where they went straight from the station to the wharf, and thence on board the steamer, which an hour or so afterwards cast off from her moorings and steamed out of the harbour.

*   *   *   *

A few weeks later Captain Grey received a cheque from Mrs. Reynard in full payment of the passage-money, together with a sweet little note in which that lady prettily expressed her contrition at the un-warrantable manner in which she had deceived him, and her concern at the indignity to which he had been subjected, pleading as an excuse the stern necessity of the occasion, and entreating his forgive-ness for her naughty little trick, and quite too shameful behaviour.

OUR STATION.

THE term as applied to Sandriri is a misnomer, there is nothing whatever stationary about it. Here even mere molecular change is accelerated; the roads oscillate violently between a state of disruption and repair; our public buildings, of which we are so proud, are for ever drifting from a condition justifying popular reprehension and alarm to one of successful re-cuperation and general joy; while our dwelling-houses either totter, cracked and tarnished, to their fall, or, just " done up," stand, white-robed candidates for the lodger sufferage. The very name of our mobile burgh is the victim of unrest. Within the recollection of the least retentive memory it was familiarly known among men as Sundreary, and we are only now beginning to get reconciled to seeing our old friend caricatured in print as Sandriri. But here there is a schism among us. The Judge is uncom-promisingly for the new jargon, and in this he

Q

receives the support of the salt-wallah and the Statutory ; but the Collector, except when he is penning an official document, when even *he* bows the knee to Rimmon, adheres sturdily to the old rendering, and his manful protest commands the respectful approval of the Doctor, the Policeman, and me. This rift within the lute is widening, but it does not as yet effect our social intercourse; after all, it is a small matter—Sandriri, like the rose, will under any other name exhale the same odours.

But this is a digression. Sandriri is not a station, it is a mirage, a fluxion, a dream. Its society is constantly changing; if not actually on the wing, we are all preening our feathers for a flight; not a man of us is *pucka*, all are acting for some one else. We are like marionettes suspended by metallic threads, the Chief Secretary touches our wire, and off we skip to a distant corner of the stage, and hang, quivering with expectation, awaiting our next removal. Shakespeare had us in his eye when he declared all the world to be a stage. But our stage-world is a work-a-day one; though "vagrom" men, we are no rascal players; we are actors in the sense only that we are all waiting for the *Gazette's* call-bell to ring our

successors on. Each house has its price-list ready
for issue; every particular in these price-lists is
familiar to each of us, for it has long ago been
exhaustively discussed in racket-court and club-
room, and each item has been conclusively appraised.
Though we attend auctions as regularly as we attend
church, nobody ever buys anything; for what is the
use of residual tubs and sedimentary dog-carts to a
man who to-morrow may find himself in orders for
Jerichobad?

Another marked feature in our condition is the
pleasureable sunshine of anticipation in which we
bask. All of us being in the pupa stage of official
existence, we are naturally expectant of a glorious
transformation when we rend our present husk.
Each has a splendid future dancing on his mental
retina, and the humblest among us cherishes the
hope of a gorgeous development. Although we do
not confide these precious anticipations to one
another categorically, we dimly hint at them in
after-dinner dialogue, or embody them in vague
references over a cheroot. We therefore know
as much about our neighbour's prospects as we
do about his property. Thus we are all aware that
the Collector is calmly expectant of honours from

afar, and that any day may see him invested with highly-coveted distinctions. Even our Zemindar, who believes that the world rests upon a tortoise, knows this. The following beautifully-expressed sentiment adorns and terminates the last letter that the Collector received from this Eastern nobleman : "May the inexhaustible British Alphabet discharge its choicest treasures on the brow of the Humphrey Buckley, and may neither of the precious triads (C. S. I. and C. I. E.) be absent from the chaplet." Without going quite so far as our Statutory Civilian, it must be admitted that our Collector's accession will add lustre even to the ranks of the three lettered men. It may be observed that with our Statutory, admiration of the District Chief has grown into a cult. He describes him as a man whom merely to know is a middle-school training ; whom to be fairly well acquainted with is a Madras University course ; but to be honoured with whose intimate confidence confers an encyclopædic education, boundless in extent and unfathomable in profundity. Our Statutory is a poet. In addition to a poem containing one thousand and odd verses laudatory of Vishnu, he has written " Lines in Honour of the Planet Saturn," " A Centum of Verse in Praise of the Victorious

Rama," " A Standard Poem on the Merit of a Vow
to Siva on the Evening of the Twelfth Day of each
Fortnight," illustrated by the legend of a Prince
who, by his strict observance of the oath, was blessed
with all possible mundane prosperity. Last Christmas he hailed the Collector in the spirited verses
here subjoined :—

> Who makes dakait and thag to quail
> At thoughts of cat of poly-tail,
> And kanji fare in District jail ?
> Kallecta.

> Who is it that with lightning blow
> Lays the striated tiger low,
> Fox, vulture, jackal, snipe, and crow ?
> Kallecta.

> Who when the small-pox smote the town
> Urged his career in bagi brown
> And cast zymotic structures down ?
> Kallecta.

> Who brings monsún's prolific rain,
> Fecundates fields with grass and grain,
> With calves and kidlings throngs the plain ?
> Kallecta.

> Who when Lard-Governor H. E.
> Arrived by dák, all things to see,
> With him ate rice, with him drank tea ?
> Kallecta.

Who, worthy of Valmiki's lays,
Reckless of censure as of praise,
Gives good appointments to B.A.'s ?
                                  Kallecta.

Who scorns the potent argent lure,
Contemns the vile, supports the pure ?
Long may his clement rule endure,
                                  Kallecta.

The Collector ministers to our spiritual requirements by reading us a sermon every Sunday, and
attends to our corporal wants by giving us a dinner
afterwards for listening to him.

Our Judge has his eye upon the High Court, and
it is believed that the High Court has its eye upon him;
several of his decisions having lately been severely
reversed upon appeal. Yet he is a man of whom all,
saving the Policeman, speak well, and the bobby's
growl is confined to session-time. The motto is trite,
"Cum nocens absolvitur judex damnatur," by the
Superintendent of Police.

The Policeman is a meritorious person, well acquainted with courts and scamps, and many a tangled
web can weave round him whose practice is to thieve.
We like him ; his helmet alone inspires us with confidence, its scarlet turban reflects the blushes of the
detected rogue, while the spike and chain, eloquent

emblems of the Bastile, are a standing menace to evil-doers.

Our Doctor aspires to the management of the Powder Factory. He is much respected in the station, for in his hands lie priceless possibilities—leave in India, to Australia, to Europe lurks within the wrinkles of his unfee'd palm. His favourite axioms are that blue water beats blue pill, and that leave is better than leeches. We applaud these tenets, their adoption by our medical adviser commands our warm and sympathetic approval, and we heartily encourage him in their freest translation into practice.

I must not forget to mention that the district contains an Assistant-Collector, one Spraggin. He is a Socinian or a Socialist, I forget which, and he writes epigrams, and admires George (not the Duke), and I don't know what. He sneers at everything, and has been heard to speak disrespectfully even of the tropics; we have therefore dubbed him *Pooh-bah*. We do not esteem this young man.

Much interest was excited one morning, when at our usual rendezvous in the Judge's verandah, Buckley, without the slightest preparatory proem, announced that the French Academy of Science had

despatched a *savant* to India in order to observe the
approaching osculation of Venus, a subject that was
creating no little stir among the astronomers of the
northern hemisphere, and that the place selected as
in all respects most favourable for the observation was
Sandriri.

That day five letters were privately indited and
secretly despatched to a bookseller in Madras. And
in the course of the week the post-peon distributed
among us five packets, each contained (for, after our
usual manner, we confessed it afterwards) a French
grammar and a *Manuel de phrases*.

Our visitor, Chevalier Achile Hypolite Dumaresq,
was an officer of the Legion of Honour, a Member of
the Institute, a Professor of the Collége de France, a
Lecturer of the Athénée, and a Fellow of half the
scientific and literary bodies in Europe. The care of
such a distinguished person could devolve upon only
one man. The Chevalier, in the order of nature,
became the guest of the Collector.

The day after his arrival, the station was summoned
to a banquet in his honour. It might have been
observed that we were all deeply absorbed in thought,
and had the air of men trying not to lose the recollection of something. The Chevalier spoke but little

English, and that was of an inferior quality; it was therefore tacitly understood that the conversation was to be in French.

We consumed the soup in silence, and although the Chevalier addressed several remarks to the company at large we only smiled and bowed, we were waiting for Buckley to begin. I had learnt two beautiful sentences from the *Manuel*, and had skilfully adapted them to the present occasion. Suddenly Buckley gave a preparatory cough; we listened intently.

" Il fait bien chaud aujourd'hui, Monsieur le Chevalier."

This from the Collector did not come up to our expectations, but it sufficed to tap the pent-up stream of the foreigner's loquacity. At the first lull the Judge delivered his little speech :

" N'est ce pas que vous trouvez la chaleur des Indes accablante ? "

Again the Chevalier went off at score. By this time the champagne had been twice round, and the Doctor, the Policeman, and I began to pluck up courage. I could see by the anxiety depicted on the countenances of my neighbours that they were going to strike in, so, with my usual modesty, I reserved my remark.   In their eagerness they both spoke together.

"On vous attendait, Monsieur, la semaine dernière, le temps n'était pas si lourd et des brises légères entretiennent une douce fraîcheur."

Misery! that was one of mine.   Off again went the Chevalier, addressing either speaker alternately. They listened with facile nods and hypocritical grins —the impostors! as though they understood him. At last he put a direct question to the Doctor, to which that worthy with a ghastly smile responded: "Mais oui."

"Comment!" inquired the Chevalier, with an air of surprise dashed with horror.   There was a dead silence.   The Doctor had evidently gone wrong.

"Do I comprehend you to say zat you have here ze peste, ze plague?"

"Non, non, non," said the Doctor, blushing, "pas le plague, mais maintenant et puis le choléra."

Our spirits rose at the Doctor's discomfiture; his ignorance presented a good background for our own more brilliant scholarship, and we listened with great good-humour, albeit with imperfect comprehension, to the Chevalier's account of the ravages of the plague at Jaffa and Beyrout.

There was then a short silence. The others had shot their bolt, and it was now my turn for an innings. With an air of proud humility I delivered myself, my companions listening critically.

"Nous avons eu beaucoup de moustiques ici, Monsieur, et il faisait chaud. Par bleu! bien chaud."

This unfortunately led to a complicated question about our Indian seasons, and the extent of country affected by the monsoon. Being most anxious to impart to my inquirer the exact limit of the rainfall to a fraction, I referred in English to Buckley, and then found myself engaged in conversation with the Policeman about a small case in which I suddenly remembered that I was profoundly interested.

In the middle of dinner, who should turn up but Spraggin, who, being a mathematical genius, had been called in to assist the Chevalier at the osculation. Buckley would not hear of his delaying to change his coat, but made him join us in his riding-gear. He sat opposite the Chevalier and at once engaged him in an animated conversation. His powers of speech were marvellous, he positively rippled over with French, and spoke it with the ease and grace of the

Chevalier himself; moreover, he had the Gallic shrug to perfection, and to our untutored eyes and ears his accent was as Parisian as his gestures.

We always disliked the Assistant Collector for his absurd affectation of superiority, but that night we detested him. Even Buckley seemed annoyed. Spraggin and Dumaresq spoke so fast that we could not follow them, and we were too much dazzled by this manifestation of a new power on the part of the former to talk much among ourselves, so we finished our dinner in silence, and felt it a relief when we adjourned to the verandah for cigars, leaving Spraggin and the Chevalier hard at it on a point, as it seemed to me, of astronomy, but Buckley said they were talking about protoplastic generation.

It turned out afterwards that their dialogue had reference to the *demi-monde* of Vienna.

HOW WE JUBILATED AT SANDRIRI.

"I suppose we must have a meeting?" observed the Judge.

"Undoubtedly," replied the Collector, and the word was echoed by the Doctor, the Policeman, and me.

We were all seated in the Collector's verandah, drinking early tea.

"Of course," remarked the first speaker, lighting a long cheroot—"of course we must have the Zemindar."

"We *must* have the Zemindar," said the Collector authoritatively.

"We *must* have the Zemindar," was the unanimous remark.

Let it not be thought that we were servile followers of the Collector. We loved him and admired him, and he, being a man of masterful mind, *appeared* to lead us.

" And Soucar Laksha Paisa too," added the Judge.

" Very much so," answered the Collector, with the magisterial analogue of a wink.

The Doctor, the Policeman, and I also winked as magisterially as we could, and laughed sarcastically at the bare idea of excluding the local Rothschild from deliberations of which a leading feature would be the question of supply.

" Then I'll communicate with old R. P.," said the Collector, taking a blue pencil and an envelope from his waistcoat pocket.

R. P., signified Ramia Puntalu, the district Sheristadar.

" And I'll tell him to have a subscription-list handy." This remark, it is needless to say, was, like every other wise suggestion, readily endorsed by the Doctor, the Policeman, and me.

The meeting was held that day week, and was attended by a numerous and enthusiastic company, *vide* R. P.'s report in the local journal.

Of course we were all there. The Judge, the Collector, the Policeman, the Zemindar, the Doctor, the Soucar, the whole box and dice of us, besides a phalanx of fifteen native gentlemen marshalled and inspired by the venerable R. P.

The Collector's speech was an immense success, eliciting in its more serious portions frequent and prolonged applause, and provoking in its lighter sallies bursts of exuberant merriment. The young native gentleman, who held and adorned the position of Statutory Civilian, showed himself on this occasion to be endowed with a truly abnormal sense of humour; and what was of infinitely greater importance, both the Zemindar and Laksha Paisa displayed an earnest interest in the proceedings.

The speech concluded by an eloquent appeal to the liberality of the audience, representing, as it did, all the rank, wealth, and solid respectability of the town and its neighbourhood, an audience which, the speaker was satisfied, needed no incitement from him to support the undertaking in a manner worthy alike of the occasion, of themselves, and of the ancient renown of Sandriri.

We applauded the orator to the echo, and when the Judge proposed that an address should be forwarded to Her Majesty from her loyal and grateful Sandririans, we with one accord named our Collector as the fittest person to draw it up.

The Zemindar, speaking through his agent, suggested that the address should be enclosed in a gold casket, and the Soucar added a rider that the the box should be incrusted with diamonds, incidentally remarking that he himself dealt largely in precious stones.

These proposals were followed by others equally bountiful and large-hearted, and the Collector, noting the fervid state of generosity into which the meeting had worked itself, made a sign to R. P., who produced the subscription-list.

We raised exactly a thousand rupees, the sum being made up as follows:—

	Rs.
M. R. Ry. The Zemindar of Sandriri	500
The Judge	150
The Collector	150
The Doctor	50
The Supt. of Police	50
I	50
R. P.	25
Fourteen Native Gentlemen	14
Our Statutory	6
Soucar Laksha Paisa	5

N.B.—The last donation has not yet been paid.

We then formed a committee to decide how we should spend the funds. As all present were subscribers, to exclude any of us would have been invidious, so we voted ourselves into committee and set to work.

After some slight consultation it was agreed that our address should be transmitted to Her Majesty in a government envelope, instead of in a box, the former being a more natural vehicle for the conveyance of printed matter. We then began our resolutions.

The first proposition, moved by R. P., and seconded enthusiastically by the Statutory, was that we should erect a pandal.

At Sandriri nothing festive can be accomplished without the aid of a pandal. Whenever Sandriri rejoices, the effluence and symbol of its gladness takes the form of bamboos and palm-leaves, fruit-bearing plantain-trees, and margosa-leaves tied to horizontal strings. We carried the pandal unanimously. It was at once cheap and effective, and was strictly in accordance with tradition.

The second proposal also was carried *nem. con.*— we were to have fireworks.

The third proposal emanated from the Zemindar. It was that we should have a locomotive battle after the manner of a ram-fight. Two opposing engines

R

launched at full speed were to meet in front of
the railway station, where the assembled company
would be seated under a pandal, of course a pandal, to
witness and perhaps experience the effect.

This suggestion was negatived as one tending to
lead to a massacre of the spectators.

The fourth proposal was that Her Imperial
Majesty's picture should be placed upon the Zemindar's rhinoceros, the animal being decked out with
lotuses and lured through the town by means of
sweetmeats, while all the most respectable nautch-
girls available danced in front.   A difficulty was here
encountered.   The Zemindar at once most obligingly
placed his rhinoceros at our disposal, and R. P.
undertook to provide the dancing-girls; but none of
us was fortunate enough to possess a copy of the
Imperial picture, so it was decided to affix a new
rupee to an ebony board and to place it on a velvet
cushion in a covered howdah, which was to be carried
by the garlanded rhinoceros under the shadow of
gilded umbrellas.

We were also to have sports.   There were military
pensioners in the town, and these were under the
control of the Collector, so R. P. was instructed to
arrange an assault-at-arms.

Here we paused; it was felt that our resources would not carry us much further, and when somebody proposed that "something of a permanent nature" should be undertaken for the good of the town, we did not like it, for it savoured of a supplementary subscription list. However, the question having been started, various plans were presented for discussion.

The Soucar, having a piece of ground that he wanted to get rid of, proposed to create a Jubilee cemetery. This notion was rejected on the score of extravagance—the station burial-ground not being yet full. The Statutory Civilian suggested that a picture of the Collector should be hung in the Cutcherry. This was a good proposal, but it was promptly negatived by the officer in question before either the Doctor, the Policeman, or I could rise to our feet to second it.

It occurred to me that I should like to have a Jubilee pension, but I refrained from proposing it, fearing to incur the reproach of avidity.

The Superintendent then advocated the establishment of a Jubilee lock-up; the Doctor proposed a branch-hospital; some one else wanted to have a bridge over a nullah that was dry eleven months in the year, and seldom full during the twelfth ; a fourth person considered Sandriri incomplete without a triumphal arch ; while a fifth insisted upon the unique grace and beauty of an obelisk. All these proposals had been successively debated and rejected, when R. P., having gone into private committee of ways and means at an old desk in the corner, came forward and announced that after meeting the expenses already voted, we should have in hand only some twenty rupees, and to achieve even that result we should have to curtail the supply of sweetmeats to the rhinoceros ; so at the instance of the Collector, supported by the Doctor, the Policeman, the Statutory, and me, we decided upon confining ourselves to the erection of—a Jubilee Pump.

*   *   *   *

The sports were not an unqualified success. The Zemindar had lent us all his elephants, and we went in procession to a neighbouring plain, which had been selected as the best theatre for the tournament.

The Zemindar, preceded by spearmen, led the way on a black monster with bells fastened to its hammer-cloth, and a fine yellow-wash of ochre on its forehead. The Collector and the Judge, each in red howdahs, and also accompanied by spearmen, were carried side by side by two quadrupeds that would have put Jumbo himself to shame ; while the Doctor, the Policeman, and I brought up the rear in an old shooting howdah borne by an undersized hathni.*

We had no retinue.

On our arrival at the ground we were met by R. P., who, with a somewhat crestfallen air, announced to the Collector that he had been unable to discover " many " military pensioners who were in a condition to perform great feats of arms, but he had procured three veterans who had been noted champions at military gatherings in days of yore.

The days of their vigour were, however, a little too much of yore ; one of the athletes, it turned out, had, just before our arrival, been suddenly affected with rheumatic pains in the knee-joints, and the other had as suddenly found himself suffering from vertigo, but they helped to swell the body of spectators. The assembly consisted of ourselves, the spearmen,

---

* Female elephant.

the Cutcherry peons, and the mahouts, before whom the remaining pensioner, who was an active old man for his years, went very creditably through the sword exercise; he then writhed round some old clubs, and leapt painfully over a stick held at a low elevation. Stimulated by our plaudits and by R. P.'s whispered announcement of coming reward, his invalid comrades now arose, and, slapping their withered biceps, grappled convulsively together in a species of gladiatorial contest, which, R. P. told us, was a wrestling match. In this struggle, although it was maintained for over sixty seconds, neither combatant was overpowered.

The three athletes then formed line, and making their obeisance to the company, received each a guerdon of two rupees from the Collector, and a packet of sweetmeats from R. P. With this the display terminated.

The rhinoceros-march afforded unalloyed pleasure to all beholders, although to some extent our pro-gramme was departed from. The beast was to have perambulated all the chief thoroughfares of the town, halting at intervals and emitting at each halt a loud grunt expressive of loyalty and devotion to the British Raj; but having got to the end of the first street, the pachyderm stopped, and although cheerfully accepting the confectionery that was lavished upon it, refused contumaciously either to grunt or to proceed a step further on its pilgrimage. The creature, moreover, began to eat its lotuses. The driver stood near with a formidable goad, which, however, he did not deem it prudent to apply. When the comestibles and the lotuses were consumed, the ungrateful unicorn turned round and solemnly carried back the Queen's image to his stable.

Upon this the Collector very happily remarked that it was the first time in the history of the town that any difficulty had been found in circulating coin of the realm.

The pandal was a charming structure, and cost us a trifle over five-hundred rupees ; while the fireworks ran us on far into the thousand, but they were very good, and made a tremendous noise and no end of smoke.

The Zemindar came late, thereby losing the best of the display ; but the Collector, the Judge, the Policeman, the Doctor and I, each of us with a large garland of yellow flowers round his neck, a gilded lime in one hand, and a small bouquet tied to a stick in the other, sat in state in the front row, while R. P.

sprinkled us at intervals, as though we were plants, with a weak solution of rose-water and cloves.

The great feature of the evening was a large transparency of the Queen-Empress copied from her effigy on the new postage stamps, the heads of the Judge and the Collector appeared on each side of her, and the inscription " God defend our rulers" blazed in large letters underneath; but the wind blew out all the second word with the exception of the first letter, and thus the effect of the sentiment was marred.

When the Zemindar arrived, he was received affectionately by us all, and was placed on a silken couch between the Collector and the Judge, where he sat for an hour in silence and chewed cardamoms. During this period a native musician discoursed Hindu melodies on a small fiddle.

Then the Collector rose and read the address, which we all vociferously applauded, while the fiddler struck up the national anthem. After this the Judge thanked the Collector for all the trouble that he had taken, and the Collector in a graceful speech thanked the Judge for all the trouble that *he* had taken; and the Doctor, on behalf of every one present, thanked the Superintendent of Police for his efficient arrangements, and particularly for his admirably successful precautions against fire. At this moment a rocket fell on the roof, and we adjourned somewhat precipitately to the street. When the fire had burnt itself out, the Police Superintendent thanked the Doctor and acknowledged the justice of his kind remarks. R. P. then thanked the European gentlemen for their attendance, and I thanked Heaven that it was all over.

We then gave three cheers, and under copious showers of rose-water rained upon us by the zealous Statutory and the indefatigable R. P., the jubilation ended. When we got home we found that we had all been severely " burgled." There had been a Jubilee jail-delivery that morning : the heaviest sufferers were the Doctor, the Police Superintendent. and I.

THE END.

Henderson & Spalding (Limited), Printers, Marylebone Lane, W.

October, 1893.

MESSRS.
LAWRENCE & BULLEN'S

List of Publications.

CONTENTS.

NEW AND FORTHCOMING BOOKS.

ALLEN, GRANT.— SCIENCE IN ARCADY.
Crown 8vo. 5*s.*
> "Holiday papers of a naturalist. The love of the country is in them all."—*Speaker.*

ANACREON.—The Greek Text, with THOMAS STANLEY'S Translation. Edited by A. H. BULLEN. Illustrated by J. R. WEGUELIN. Fcap. 4to. £1 1*s. net.*

ANDERSEN, HANS CHRISTIAN. — THE LITTLE MERMAID, AND OTHER STORIES. Translated by R. NISBET BAIN. With 65 Illustrations (chiefly full-page) by J. R. WEGUELIN. Royal 4to. 12*s. 6d.*
> * Also 150 copies on hand-made paper, with the illustrations mounted on Japanese paper.

BARRETT, C. R. B.—ESSEX: HIGHWAYS, BY-WAYS, AND WATERWAYS. First and Second Series. Written and Illustrated by C. R. B. BARRETT. (With 18 full-page etchings, and upwards of 200 drawings.) 2 vols. 12*s. 6d. net* per volume.
> * 120 copies on fine paper, with additional etchings. Price £1 11*s. 6d. net* per volume.
> "An excellent and original work."—*Athenæum.*

BARRETT, C. R. B.—ILLUSTRATED GUIDES.

1. SOUTHWOLD. *6d.*
2. ALDEBURGH. *6d.*
3. ST. OSYTH, WIVENHOE, FINGRINGHOE, and BRIGHTLINGSEA. *6d.*
4. SOUTHEND, HADLEIGH, ROCHFORD, &c. *6d.*
5. IPSWICH, HARWICH, &c. *6d.*
6. GREAT YARMOUTH. *6d.*
7. CAISTER CASTLE. *3d.*
8. ST. OSYTH PRIORY. *3d.*
9. COLCHESTER. *6d.*

"Carefully written, well printed, and amply illustrated.—*Manchester Guardian.*

BECKFORD, WILLIAM. — VATHEK. Edited by DR. RICHARD GARNETT. With 8 full-page Etchings by HERBERT NYE. Demy 8vo. £1 1s. *net.*

* 600 copies printed for England and America. Also 70 copies on Japanese vellum, with an additional etching.

BOCCACCIO, GIOVANNI. — THE DECAMERON. Translated by JOHN PAYNE. Illustrated by LOUIS CHALON. 2 vols. Imp. 8vo. £3 3s. *net.* (With 20 full-page Illustrations.)

* 1,000 copies printed for England and America.

BULLEN, A. H.—ANTHOLOGIES.

LYRICS FROM ELIZABETHAN SONG-BOOKS. Revised edition. Fcp. 8vo. 5s.

LYRICS FROM ELIZABETHAN DRAMATISTS. Revised edition. Fcp. 8vo. 5s.

BULLEN, A. H.—ANTIENT DROLLERIES, in Six Parts. 3*s.* 6*d.* per Part *net.*

> * Parts I, II, and III. "Cobbe's Prophecies," "Pymlico, or Runne Redcap," and "Quips upon Questions," have appeared. Other Parts are in active preparation. The edition consists of 300 copies.

CATULLUS.—Edited by S. G. Owen, Senior Student of Christ Church. Illustrated by J. R. Weguelin. Fcp. 4to. 16*s. net.*

> * Also 110 copies on Japanese vellum, with an additional illustration. Price £1 11*s.* 6*d. net.*

CHURCHILL, CHARLES.—ROSCIAD. Edited, with an Introduction and Notes, by Robert W. Lowe. With Portraits. Royal 4to. £1 1*s. net.*

> * The edition consists of 400 numbered copies.
>
> "The edition is not only good, but magnificent."— *Guardian.*

CHURCHILL, CHARLES. — PORTFOLIO OF PORTRAITS. 25*s. net.*

CRANE, WALTER.— CLAIMS OF DECORATIVE ART. Fcp. 4to. 7*s.* 6*d. net.*

> "No one has a better right than Mr. Walter Crane to write about the *Claims of Decorative Art,* for he is certainly one of the best masters of decorative design whom we have had among us for many a long day. . . . The book is admirably 'got up,' and does credit to the publishers."—*World.*

D'AULNOY, MADAME.—FAIRY TALES. Newly Translated into English, with an Introduction by ANNE THACKERAY RITCHIE, and Illustrations by CLINTON PETERS. Fcp. 4to. 7s. 6d.

> "An admirable gift book for girls and boys."— *National Observer.*
>
> "An exceedingly pleasing Volume." — *Saturday Review.*
>
> * *Prospectus,* with specimen plate, on application.

DAVIDSON, JOHN. — SENTENCES AND PARAGRAPHS. 18mo. 3s. 6d.

EARLE, A. M.— CHINA - COLLECTING IN AMERICA. With Illustrations. Fcp. 4to. 16s.

EDMONDS, MRS.—THE HISTORY OF A CHURCH MOUSE. A modern Greek story. Crown 8vo. 1s. 6d.

> "A graceful story, and one, moreover, which incidentally throws considerable light on the manners and customs of the Greek peasants in the more sequestered regions of that beautiful country at the present time." —*Speaker.*

GIFT, THEO.—FAIRY TALES FROM THE FAR EAST, Illustrated by O. VON GLEHN. Fcp. 4to. 5s.

> 'A charming volume adapted from the ' Birth Stories of Buddha,' as Englished by Professor Rhys Davies, with admirable drawings by Otto von Glehn."—*Saturday Review.*

GIFT, THEO.—AN ISLAND PRINCESS. A novel. 1 vol. Crown 8vo. 5s.

GISSING, GEORGE.—THE ODD WOMEN. A novel. 3 vols. 31s. 6d.

GISSING, GEORGE.—DENZIL QUARRIER. A novel. 1 vol. 6s.

GISSING, GEORGE.—THE EMANCIPATED. A novel. 1 vol. 6s. [*New and cheaper Edition.*

HARRADEN, BEATRICE.—SHIPS THAT PASS IN THE NIGHT. A novel. 1 vol. Crown 8vo. 3s. 6d. [*Fourth Edition.*

JÓKAI, MAURUS.—EYES LIKE THE SEA. A Romance. Translated from the Hungarian by R. NISBET BAIN. 3 vols. Crown 8vo. 31s. 6d.

KNIGHT, JOSEPH. — THEATRICAL NOTES (1874-1880). A contribution towards the History of the Modern English Stage. Demy 8vo. 6s.

    * Also 250 large-paper copies, with portraits of eminent actors and actresses.

LINTON, W. J.—EUROPEAN REPUBLICANS. Recollections of Mazzini and his Friends. Demy 8vo. 10s. 6d.

    " The book is one that cannot be read without some amount of searching of heart, for however our range of view, our political instincts have developed since '48, it would to-day be hard to find (save perhaps among the Russian and Polish exiles) so single-minded, unselfish, and devoted a band of politicians as these men, whom Mr. Linton revered in their lives and has fitly honoured after their death."—*Manchester Guardian.*

LINTON, W. J.—THE FLOWER AND THE STAR, and other Stories for Children. Written and Illustrated by W. J. LINTON. Fcp. 8vo. 3*s*. 6*d*.

" Delightfully fresh and unaffected. . . . The beautiful little woodcuts by the author form the most appropriate and expressive illustrations of such simple and pleasing stories that could be desired.—*Saturday Review.*

LINTON, W. J. — CATONINETALES. A Domestic Epic, by HATTIE BROWN, a young lady of colour lately deceased at the age of 14. Edited and Illustrated by W. J. LINTON. Demy 8vo. 7*s*. 6*d. net.* (330 copies printed.)

" The cat in the bag, on p. 48, though small, is too terrible."—*Saturday Review.*

MISCELLANIES—Bibliographical and Historical.

THE DIALOGUS OR COMMUNYNG BETWIXT THE WYSE KING SALOMON AND MARCOLPHUS. Reproduced in facsimile by the Oxford University Press from the unique copy of the edition printed by GERARD LEEU about 1492. Edited by E. GORDON

DUFF. Small 4to. 10s. 6d. net. (350 copies printed.)

> "Mr. Duff's edition possesses in a singular degree all the qualities which are necessary to justify a facsimile reprint."—*Guardian.*

ANTONIO DE GUARAS; OR, THE ACCESSION OF QUEEN MARY: being the Contemporary Narrative of Antonio de Guaras, a Spanish Merchant resident in London. Edited, with an Introduction, by RICHARD GARNETT, LL.D. Sm. 4to. 10s. 6d. net. (350 copies printed.)

> " On the interest and importance of the narrative itself it is needless to dwell. . . . It is equally needless to say that Dr. Garnett has discharged his functions as editor in a masterly fashion."—*Times.*

SEX QUAM ELEGANTISSIME EPISTOLE IMPRESSE PER WILLELUM CAXTON ET DILIGENTER EMENDATE PER PETRUM CARMELIANUM. Reproduced in facsimile by JAMES HYATT. Edited, with a Translation, by GEORGE BULLEN, C.B., LL.D. Sm. 4to. 10s. 6d. net. (350 copies printed.)

> "As a specimen of Caxtonian typography—and, we may add, of its artistic reproduction by means of photographic lithography—no less than on account of Dr. Bullen's exegetic labours, this reprint will be accounted curious and valuable."—*Times.*

INFORMACON FOR PYLGRYMES: Reproduced in facsimile by the Oxford University

Press from the unique copy preserved in the Advocates' Library at Edinburgh. Edited by E. GORDON DUFF. Sm. 4to. 10s. 6d. *net.* (350 copies printed.)

    * A prospectus of the *Miscellanies* will be sent on application.

MUSES' LIBRARY—

POEMS OF WILLIAM BROWNE, OF TAVISTOCK. Edited by GORDON GOODWIN, with an Introduction by A. H. BULLEN. 2 vols. 18mo. 10s. *net.*

POEMS OF WILLIAM BLAKE. Edited by W. B. YEATS. 1 vol. 18mo. 5s. *net.*

POEMS OF JOHN DONNE. Edited by E. K. CHAMBERS, with an Introduction by GEORGE SAINTSBURY. 2 vols. 18mo. 10s. *net.*

    VOLUMES OF THE SERIES ALREADY ISSUED.

WORKS OF ROBERT HERRICK. Edited by A. W. POLLARD. With a Preface by A. C. SWINBURNE. 2 vols. 18mo. 10s. *net.*

POEMS AND SATIRES OF ANDREW MARVELL. Edited by G. A. AITKEN. 2 vols. 18mo. 10s. *net.*

POEMS OF EDMUND WALLER. Edited by G. THORN DRURY. 1 vol. 18mo. 5s. *net.*

POEMS OF JOHN GAY. Edited by J. UNDERHILL. 2 vols. 18mo. 10s. *net.*

    * Also 200 large-paper copies.
    † Other volumes of the series are in active preparation.

O'NEILL, MOIRA.—AN EASTER VACATION. A story. Crown 8vo. 3s. 6d.

ORME, TEMPLE. — MATRICULATION CHEMISTRY. Small 8vo. 2s. 6d.

ORME, TEMPLE.—RUDIMENTS OF CHEMISTRY. Small 8vo. 2s. 6d.

OWEN, J. A. (Editor of "On Surrey Hills," &c.) WOODLAND WAYS. Crown 8vo. 3s. 6d.

PEARCE, J. H. (Author of "Esther Pentreath," &c.) DROLLS FROM SHADOWLAND. 18mo. 3s. 6d.

POWELL, G. H.—OCCASIONAL RHYMES AND REFLECTIONS. Demy 8vo. Boards, 1s. 6d. Cloth, 2s.

"Mr. Powell may fairly claim to share with Mr. Traill the laurels of modern English pasquinade."—*Times.*

PRIDEAUX, MISS S. T.—HISTORICAL SKETCH OF BOOKBINDING. (With a chapter "ON STAMPED BINDINGS," by E. GORDON DUFF.) Sm. 4to. 6s. net.

* Also 120 copies (numbered) on fine paper, with two facsimiles specially prepared by Mr. Griggs. £1 1s. net.

"We propose to consider the subject as it falls naturally into three main periods : the first from 1494, when Aldus Manutius had his printing press at Venice, to the end of the 16th century. This was the period of Maioli and Grolier, of the royal bindings done for Francis I. and Henri II. The art attained almost at once its highest perfection, at all events from the point of view of

design. Secondly, the 17th century, with which are
associated the names of the Eves and Le Gascon.
Thirdly, the 18th century, the time of Boyat, Duseuil,
Nicolas, and Antoine Padeloup and the Deromes, in
France, and of the Harleian style and Roger Payne in
England. Any division must necessarily be somewhat
arbitrary, but it happens that in this case the centuries
correspond pretty definitely to the different types of the
art at different periods of its development."

RABELAIS, FRANCIS. — THE WORKS OF MASTER FRANCIS RABELAIS. Translated by Sir THOMAS URQUHART, of Cromarty, and PETER ANTONY MOTTEUX. With an Introduction by ANATOLE DE MONTAIGLON. Illustrated by L. CHALON. 2 vols. Imp. 8vo. £3 3s. net.

1,000 copies for England and America.

* *Prospectus*, with specimen plate, will be sent on
application.

The copious racy vocabulary of Urquhart's "Rabelais," the odd quirks and flourishes, the gusto and swing
of the rollicking narrative, can never fail to delight liberal
readers.

The publishers of the present edition claim to have
dealt handsomely with Rabelais and Sir Thomas
Urquhart. They invited a very distinguished French
artist, Mons. L. Chalon, to paint a series of oil-colour
illustrations, which have been reproduced by Dujardin.
The originals were lately exhibited at the "Blanc et Noir,"
Paris, where they were awarded a First Medal.

Prefixed to the translation is an essay on Rabelais
(specially written for this edition) by a scholar of European
reputation, M. Anatole de Montaiglon, whose knowledge
of early French literature is certainly unsurpassed and
probably unequalled. Facsimiles of rare title-pages of
early French editions accompany the Introduction.

The volumes are printed by Messrs. Whittingham in
the best style of the Chiswick Press.

ROBERTS, MORLEY.—KING BILLY OF BALLARAT, and other Tales. Crown 8vo. 5s.

" Mr. Roberts is a capital story-teller, with an incisive and dramatic style that is thoroughly individual.—*Saturday Review.*

ROBERTS, MORLEY.—SONGS OF ENERGY. Square 16mo. 5s.

ROBERTS, MORLEY.—LAND-TRAVEL AND SEA-FARING. With Illustrations by A. D. McCORMICK. Demy 8vo. 7s. 6d.

ROBERTS, MORLEY.—THE MATE OF THE VANCOUVER. Crown 8vo. 3s. 6d.

ROBERTS, CECIL.—ADRIFT IN AMERICA; OR, WORK AND ADVENTURE IN THE STATES. Edited by MORLEY ROBERTS. Demy 8vo. 5s.

ROBINSON, H. J. — COLONIAL CHRONO-LOGY: A chronology of the principal events connected with the English Colonies and India, from the close of the fifteenth century to the present time. With Maps. Crown folio. 16s.

" Nothing but cordial praise can be given to this valuable book."—*Manchester Guardian.*

" The book is one which ought to find a place in every library of reference."—*Speaker.*

" Admirably arranged on a plan equally simple and comprehensive." —*World.*

* *Prospectus* will be sent on application.

RUSSIAN FAIRY TALES.—Translated by R. NISBET BAIN. Illustrated by C. M. GERE. Demy 8vo. 5s. [*Second edition.*

" The very best fairy-book that we have seen this year (or indeed for many years). . . . The six admirable full-page illustrations to ' Russian Fairy Tales,' by C. M. Gere (a name quite new to us by the way), approach as near to our ideal fairy-book pictures as may be. Messrs. Lawrence & Bullen are to be congratulated on having produced the most delightful story-book of the season."— *Daily Chronicle.*

"A book to read and a book to keep.—*Pall Mall Gazette.*

" Delightfully original, naïve and humorous."— *Truth.*

SCARRON, PAUL, COMICAL WORKS. Done into English by TOM BROWN of Shifnal. With an Introduction by J. J. JUSSERAND. Illustrated from the Designs of OUDRY. 2 vols. Demy 8vo. £1 1s. *net.*

* Also 150 copies on Japanese vellum. £2 2s. *net.*

" Published in a handsome form with every luxury of type and paper. A special feature consists in the designs by Oudry, the famous dog-painter to Louis XV. These are masterpieces of spirit and taste. . . . To the knowledge elsewhere accessible concerning the book, M. Jusserand now adds a brilliant account of the author." —*Athenæum.*

STRANG, WILLIAM. — DEATH AND THE PLOUGHMAN'S WIFE. A Ballad. With 9 Etchings and 2 Mezzotint Engravings. Folio.

* The price and the number of copies will be announced shortly.

TOLD IN THE VERANDAH.—Passages in the Life of Colonel Bowlong, set down by his Adjutant. Crown 8vo. 3s. 6d.

[*Third edition.*

"Colonel Bowlong is a liar of the first water. He recks not whether he deals with tiger-stories or with his alleged noble deeds on the field of battle. His tiger-story is one of the best we have ever read."—*St. James's Gazette.*

BY THE AUTHOR OF "TOLD IN THE VERANDAH." — A BLACK PRINCE AND OTHER STORIES. Crown 8vo. 3s. 6d.

VANBRUGH, SIR JOHN.—WORKS. Edited by W. C. WARD. 2 vols. Demy 8vo. (With a Portrait.) £1 5s. net.

WALLIS, HENRY.—PERSIAN AND ORIENTAL CERAMIC ART. Parts I. and II. Folio. 14s. net.

WELLS, CHARLES.—STORIES AFTER NATURE. With a Preface by W. J. LINTON. Fcp. 8vo. 7s. 6d. net.

* The edition consists of 400 numbered copies.

"The tales, with all their rouge and frippery of form, breathe a singularly clear and upright morality, and are rich in examples of noble manhood and gracious womanhood."—*Athenæum.*

WILLS, C. J.—JOHN SQUIRE'S SECRET. A novel. 1 vol. 3s. 6d. [*New and cheaper edition.*

YEATS, W. B.—THE CELTIC TWILIGHT. 18mo. 3s. 6d.

Books published at £3 3s. net.
BOCCACCIO'S *Decameron.* 2 vols.
URQUHART'S *Rabelais.* 2 vols.

3-Vol. Novels at £1 11s. 6d.
G. GISSING'S *Odd Women.*
JÓKAI'S *Eyes Like the Sea.*

£1 5s. net.
VANBRUGH'S *Plays.* 2 vols.
PORTRAITS ILLUSTRATING
CHURCHILL'S *Rosciad.*

£1 1s. net.
ANACREON. | BECKFORD'S *Vathek.*
CHURCHILL'S *Rosciad.*
PAUL SCARRON.

16s. net.
CATULLUS.

16s.
ROBINSON'S *Colonial Chronology.*
EARLE'S *China Collecting.*

14s. net.
PARTS I. and II. OF WALLIS'S
Oriental Ceramic Art.

12s. 6d. net.
BARRETT'S *Essex.*

10s. 6d. net.
SALOMON AND MARCOLPHUS.
ANTONIO DE GUARAS.
SEX QUAM ELEGANTISSIME EPIS-
TOLE.
INFORMACŌN FOR PYLGRYMES.

10s. 6d.
LINTON'S *European Republicans.*

7s. 6d. net.
LINTON'S *Catoninetales.*
WELLS' *Stories After Nature.*
WALTER CRANE'S *Decorative Art.*

7s. 6d.
D'AULNOY'S *Fairy Tales.*
MORLEY ROBERTS' *Land Travel.*

6s. net.
MISS PRIDEAUX'S *Bookbinding.*

6s.
GISSING, G., *Denzil Quarrier.*
  „   „   *The Emancipated.*
KNIGHT'S *Theatrical Notes.*

5s. net per Volume.
WILLIAM BROWNE, of Tavistock.
WILLIAM BLAKE. | JOHN DONNE.
JOHN GAY. | ROBERT HERRICK.
ANDREW MARVELL.
EDMUND WALLER.

5s.
GRANT ALLEN'S *Science in Arcady.*
BULLEN, A. H. *Lyrics from Song-
  Books.*
BULLEN, A. H. *Lyrics from
  Dramatists.*
GIFT, THEO. *Fairy Tales.*
  „   „   *An Island Princess.*
ROBERTS, MORLEY. *King Billy.*
ROBERTS, C. *Adrift in America.*

3s. 6d. net per Part.
Antient Drolleries.

3s. 6d.
DAVIDSON'S *Sentences.*
HARRADEN'S *Ships That Pass.*
LINTON'S *Flower and the Star.*
O'NEILL'S *Easter Vacation.*
OWEN, J. A., *Woodland Ways.*
PEARCE'S *Drolls from Shadowland.*
ROBERTS' *Mate of Vancouver.*
"*Told in the Verandah.*"
"*A Black Prince.*"
WILLS' *John Squire's Secret.*
YEATS' *Celtic Twilight.*

2s. 6d.
ORME'S *Rudiments of Chemistry.*
  „   *Matriculation.*

1s. 6d.
EDMONDS, MRS., *Church Mouse.*
POWELL, G. H., *Rhymes.*

6d. and 3d.
BARRETT'S *Illustrated Guides.*

www.ingramcontent.com/pod-product-compliance
Lightning Source LLC
Chambersburg PA
CBHW020341030726
47496CB00007B/1964